Annabelle arched ⟨...⟩ ⟨...⟩ n his knees.

"This is going to be a hell of a night," she said.

"I'll do my best."

Then Annabelle twisted around and called out, "Who's there?"

The doorway to the bedroom was filled with a dark figure. Slocum tried to sit up, but the woman's weight held him down at the hips. He threw his arms around her and heaved with all his strength so they both tumbled from the bed and crashed onto the floor.

But as he lay on top of Annabelle, he knew he'd been too late. There'd been a sharp *pop!* an instant before. Slocum reached around her. His hand came away sticky with her blood.

She had been shot in the back. Shot dead.

NO LONGER PROPERTY OF
ANYTHINK LIBRARIES/
RANGEVIEW LIBRARY DISTRICT

DON'T MISS THESE
ALL-ACTION WESTERN SERIES
FROM THE BERKLEY PUBLISHING GROUP

THE GUNSMITH by J. R. Roberts

Clint Adams was a legend among lawmen, outlaws, and ladies. They called him . . . the Gunsmith.

LONGARM by Tabor Evans

The popular long-running series about Deputy U.S. Marshal Custis Long—his life, his loves, his fight for justice.

SLOCUM by Jake Logan

Today's longest-running action Western. John Slocum rides a deadly trail of hot blood and cold steel.

BUSHWHACKERS by B. J. Lanagan

An action-packed series by the creators of Longarm! The rousing adventures of the most brutal gang of cutthroats ever assembled—Quantrill's Raiders.

DIAMONDBACK by Guy Brewer

Dex Yancey is Diamondback, a Southern gentleman turned con man when his brother cheats him out of the family fortune. Ladies love him. Gamblers hate him. But nobody pulls one over on Dex . . .

WILDGUN by Jack Hanson

The blazing adventures of mountain man Will Barlow—from the creators of Longarm!

TEXAS TRACKER by Tom Calhoun

J.T. Law: the most relentless—and dangerous—manhunter in all Texas. Where sheriffs and posses fail, he's the best man to bring in the most vicious outlaws—for a price.

JAKE LOGAN

SLOCUM
AND THE
THREE FUGITIVES

JOVE BOOKS, NEW YORK

THE BERKLEY PUBLISHING GROUP
Published by the Penguin Group
Penguin Group (USA) LLC
375 Hudson Street, New York, New York 10014

USA • Canada • UK • Ireland • Australia • New Zealand • India • South Africa • China

penguin.com.

A Penguin Random House Company

SLOCUM AND THE THREE FUGITIVES

A Jove Book / published by arrangement with the author

Copyright © 2013 by Penguin Group (USA) LLC.
Penguin supports copyright. Copyright fuels creativity, encourages diverse voices,
promotes free speech, and creates a vibrant culture. Thank you for having an authorized
edition of this book and for complying with copyright laws by not reproducing, scanning,
or distributing any part of it in any form without permission. You are supporting writers
and allowing Penguin to continue to publish books for every reader.

JOVE® is a registered trademark of Penguin Group (USA) LLC.
The "J" design is a trademark of Penguin Group (USA) LLC.

For information, address: The Berkley Publishing Group,
a division of Penguin Group (USA) LLC,
375 Hudson Street, New York, New York 10014.

ISBN: 978-0-515-15386-6

PUBLISHING HISTORY
Jove mass-market edition / December 2013

PRINTED IN THE UNITED STATES OF AMERICA

10 9 8 7 6 5 4 3 2 1

Cover illustration by Sergio Giovine.

This is a work of fiction. Names, characters, places, and incidents either are the product
of the author's imagination or are used fictitiously, and any resemblance to actual persons,
living or dead, business establishments, events, or locales is entirely coincidental.
The publisher does not have any control over and does not assume any responsibility for
author or third-party websites or their content.

If you purchased this book without a cover, you should be aware that this book is
stolen property. It was reported as "unsold and destroyed" to the publisher, and neither
the author nor the publisher has received any payment for this "stripped book."

1

Gunfire echoed along the broad canyon that John Slocum was following to Taos. He drew rein and looked around. If the gunshots had come from behind him, back in the direction of Raton Pass, he would have kept riding, but the shots had come from ahead. He reached across and touched the ebony butt of his Colt Navy slung in its cross-draw holster. He didn't hunt for trouble, but it had a way of finding him.

He patted the neck of his Appaloosa stallion as much to settle his own nerves as those of the horse. The high-spirited animal reared, front hooves pawing at the air.

"Whoa, no need to get all spooked," he said. The horse calmed. Slocum remained keyed up.

He considered simply pitching camp and letting the trouble ahead fade away—and trouble it had to be since the shots came from different guns. One had a sharp crack to it. A rifle. The replying shot came flat and hollow. A pistol. Slocum perked up when he heard a new fusillade. More rifles. At least two, maybe three. The response from the six-gun ended after four shots. Slocum imagined the man with the handgun dropping behind a rock and fumbling to reload before the others rushed him.

This was no hunting party, unless the three rifles belonged to lawmen. He had a natural inclination to avoid marshals intent on arresting outlaws since it was possible those same lawmen might have seen a wanted poster on his head. Life had been rough at times, and Slocum was anything but pure as the wind-driven snow. The first warrant for his arrest came after he killed a carpetbagger judge and his henchman back at Slocum's Stand in Calhoun, Georgia. Slocum had been recovering from a gunshot to the gut he had acquired during the war, and the judge mistook his wound for weakness.

Trumping up fake tax liens had been easy enough for the judge. It hadn't been much harder for a battle-weary, battle-hardened John Slocum to put two rounds in each man, then bury them out by his springhouse. Knowing how killing a Reconstruction judge was a crime sure to bring down the federal soldiers on his neck, he had ridden west without so much as a look back.

His life had been filled with other crimes—bank robberies, stagecoach holdups, even men gunned down. Some had produced more wanted posters while other misdeeds had gone without him being identified. Mostly, he tried to keep to a lawful existence, but it proved hard at times.

He should turn around and go back through Raton Pass into Colorado and find some other destination. Nothing in Taos drew him, other than he hadn't been to the mountain town for years and it suited him right now to spend a week or two there.

Another route would take him away from the chance he'd be riding toward a posse intent on arresting an outlaw. Any other route. He rode straight ahead.

A couple miles down the road he saw how the fight progressed. Three men with rifles were arrayed at the base of a low hill. Now and then the solitary man atop the hill popped up like a prairie dog and flung lead wildly. No matter how much ammunition he had, he was a goner. The trio below him advanced in concert. One drew his fire while the other two crept farther up the hill.

Slocum watched a few minutes and came to the conclusion that the three riflemen weren't the law. No badges glinted in the sunlight, and something deep in his gut made him feel they were outlaws looking to pull a quick robbery.

The man on the hilltop kept up a steady fire but had to realize he was fighting a losing battle. Slocum rode a bit closer and saw where the horses had been tethered, two chestnuts and a paint. All carried an X Bar X brand on their hindquarters. This changed his impression of what was happening. These might be cowboys from a spread intent on running a rustler to ground.

His gut told him something else. Three outlaws, one victim.

He trotted away from the tethered horses and saw a trail leading to the summit where the lone defender made his stand. Slocum considered how stupid his snap decision was. He could have guessed wrong at every turn, and the fight raged over something beyond his imagination. But his gut refused to accept that.

He slowed his climb and finally dismounted, not wanting to risk a stray slug finding his Appaloosa. He unlimbered his Winchester and fished out a couple boxes of ammo from his saddlebags before hiking up the trail. A lathered, nervous mare told him he was getting closer.

"I'm not with them. You in trouble?" Slocum stood stock-still where the gunman could see him. "If you want me to leave, I will."

"Who are you?" The voice carried just a touch of shrillness, communicating the man's fear. "You're not with them 'shiners?"

"Don't know what you mean. I was riding by and heard the gunfire. I—"

Slocum brought his rifle to his shoulder, levered in a round, and fired. The slug ricocheted off the top of a boulder, sending rock fragments into the face of an attacker who had finally reached the summit. A bandanna pulled up in a mask protected his face but drove him back.

"You missed him," came the accusation.

"I was rushed. I'm a better shot when I take aim."

"Why'd you come up here? I don't know you."

"I don't know you either, but three *bandidos* against one looks unfair to me."

"You're not from town?"

"Taos? I'm headed there."

"Get me out of this, and I'll stand you all the whiskey you can drink. I own a saloon there."

Slocum advanced, wary of both other ambushers coming over the crest of the hill and of the man he'd befriended. He looked around the small clearing where the battle raged. Spent brass everywhere attested to the amount of ammunition expended on this side of the fight.

"They're creeping up on one side of the hill while I'm pinning them down on the other," the man said.

Slocum looked him over. He was a young man, maybe in his mid-twenties, and sported a neatly trimmed beard. The light brown was already shot with streaks of premature gray. His hat would never do to carry water again because of the holes through both the crown and the brim. In spite of the long fight, his attitude showed he was not defeated or even much fearful. Slocum appreciated that as much as he did the steadiness of the man's gun hand.

"Name's Harris, Tom Harris," the man said.

Slocum introduced himself and asked what the fight was about.

"Came up sideways against them 'shiners."

"What's that mean?"

"Moonshiners. They're trying to force me to buy their

version of Taos Lightning, the most vicious popskull ever distilled in New Mexico Territory."

"Sounds like the kind of liquor you'd want to serve," Slocum said, settling down to study the hillside. He propped his elbows on a flat rock and drew a bead at a notch in the boulders where anyone creeping up had to come. Slocum didn't have to wait but a few seconds. His round missed but drove the masked man back, scurrying for cover. "What cowboy doesn't appreciate having the top blown off his head with a single shot of liquor?"

"This stuff is deadly. Men have died drinking it. A couple cowpokes went blind. More 'n that, the 'shiners are trying to charge four times what I can get liquor for from up in Denver." Harris took a quick shot. "Trying to get up there to sign some supply contracts. Got a pocket full of cash to seal those contracts."

Harris looked hard at Slocum when he realized what he'd confessed.

"Don't worry. I've got enough money to keep me going. No need to hold you up," Slocum said.

The young man's impetuosity explaining the problem pointed out how he might have gotten into other jams. He shot off his mouth without thinking.

"Free booze at the Black Hole *and* a job if you want it," Harris promised. He rose, fired off four quick rounds.

"Get down, you fool!" Slocum shouted.

Too late. One of the men below had decoyed Harris into revealing himself. His partner took an easy shot that caught the saloon owner in the chest. Harris staggered back, then sat and looked stupidly as blood spread on his chest. Slocum swung around and fired until he worried that his barrel might melt. He ran out of rounds before that happened, but the metal smoked. The wild spray of lead failed to find a target but drove both ambushers back down the hill.

Slocum drew his Colt and got off another shot at the third

man. The slug tore at the long tan canvas duster and kicked it away from the man's body. Slocum tried to get a better idea who he faced, but other than the man being slightly built and fleet of foot, he failed to see anything but the hole he had put in the canvas.

Only when he was certain they had retreated did he go to kneel beside Tom Harris. Slocum turned grim when he saw the wound. The slug should have killed Harris outright but somehow the man hung on tenaciously to life. His brown eyes flickered open, and finally focused.

"Get me back to town. I got family I want to see before I die," Harris said.

"Keep your hand pressed down hard here," Slocum said. He whipped off his bandanna and put it over the bullet hole. "That's the way."

"You got an idea how to get out of here alive?"

Slocum nodded. The idea boiled up and appealed to him for its audacity. The trio of gunmen thought they held the upper hand, no matter that they had to keep attacking uphill. To him that showed their lack of experience or maybe their overconfidence.

"You need to fire now and then. Don't worry about hitting them. Just make it sound like there're still two of us up here."

"You going to flank 'em?"

"Something like that," Slocum said. He propped Harris up and put the rifle into his hand.

He cast a quick look back as he retreated down the hill to where he'd left his horse. The Appaloosa pawed the rocky ground, nervous over the gunfire. Slocum vaulted into the saddle and rode back down the trail, keeping an eye peeled for the ambushers. It had to occur to one of them that Slocum had found a different way to the hilltop and come hunting. But if they assaulted Harris up the steeper slope one more time, he would have time to put his plan into action.

For all the good that would do if the trio killed Harris—or

he died from the chest wound. Slocum had seen plenty of wounds during the war. The only good thing to say about the one that pushed Harris increasingly into the arms of death came in that the lead had missed puncturing a lung. He hadn't been blowing pink foam, but that meant little if he caught another bullet before Slocum returned.

Slocum got to the base of the hill and circled back to the trail he had traveled before. He spotted the road agent he had almost ventilated. The duster flapped around a thin frame and dragged the ground. Slocum wished he had his rifle, because the shot was too great for a pistol. He kept riding until he reached the three tethered horses.

He quickly gathered the reins and got the three horses trailing him as he galloped away. The noise of his departure brought all three gunmen running from where they mounted their attack. They fired but the range proved too great and Slocum's speed too fast for accurate marksmanship.

Rather than keep riding back into Colorado so many miles distant, he once more found his way to the top of the hill, where Harris still propped himself up, the Winchester balanced against a rock. He looked up with dull eyes as Slocum dismounted.

"You rode fast. Where'd you get the remuda?" Harris blinked, winced, and pressed harder into his chest. "Oh, you stole their horses. You're a caution, Slocum. Wish I'd had a chance to know you better."

"You're not dead yet," Slocum said, helping the man to a horse. It took a bit of work, but Harris finally settled in the saddle. "I need to keep them honest, for a little while, at least."

Slocum took the rifle and scanned the hillside for any movement. He fired methodically, aiming with all the skill he possessed. During the war he had been a sniper. Putting that expertise to work now forced the three attackers to cover. Only when he saw no movement from them did he step up onto his horse and start back down the steep road.

"You know a way to Taos that doesn't make us go back to the main road?"

"Keep going across country. This is a pretty mountain meadow, part of the Ortiz land grant. Nobody does anything here but graze cattle. The road curves around by the time we get to the far side. Manny Ortiz doesn't like gringos riding his land, but he'll never know."

Slocum preferred to ride along without much jawing, but he saw that it kept Harris alert. When the man stopped talking, he began to wobble in the saddle. More than once, Slocum had to fall back, reach over, and grab Tom's arm to keep the man from falling. Somehow, they made it to Taos, a quaint pueblo of closely packed adobe buildings and a plaza bustling with life.

The people, seeing Slocum with Harris, fell silent. As he rode through, they parted like water and then flowed back behind. When no one ventured to help, Slocum asked, "He needs a doctor. Where can I find him?"

A Mexican looked up with wide, round brown eyes and pointed.

"*Allí*," he said. "There. Down the street."

"*Gracias*," Slocum said, about exhausting his polite Spanish. He tugged on the reins of the horse Harris rode and the other two. When the crowd thought he was out of earshot, they began whispering.

Slocum knew instinctively that the gossip was less about the saloon owner being shot in the chest and brought to town than it was about the three horses. If he'd dallied, he might have overheard exactly what the people were saying, but getting Harris to the sawbones mattered more.

He saw the wood sign swinging in the stiff afternoon breeze and tied up the horses at a nearby hitching post. Harris fell from the saddle. Slocum caught him, staggered under the weight, and swung the man around, mostly dragging him into the doctor's office.

A man looking older than the hills blinked, adjusted his glasses, and studied Slocum for a moment.

"What are you bringing me today, young man?"

"You know him? He was ambushed by road agents outside town." Slocum swung Harris around and laid him on the table in the center of the room.

"Tom!" The doctor shot to his feet, crammed his glasses down more firmly on his nose, and pushed Slocum aside. "Let me have some light to see. My God, how are you still alive, Tom?"

"Tougher than you ever thought, Dr. Zamora. That's how."

"You didn't shoot him?" Zamora looked up over the tops of his glasses at Slocum. "No, you didn't. Why bring him in if you had." Zamora grabbed scissors and snipped away the coat, vest, and shirt matted to Harris's chest. When he discarded the coat, he hesitated. His nimble fingers pulled out a wallet bulging with greenbacks. "You could have taken his money."

"Will he make it, Doc?"

Slocum hadn't realized Harris carried so much money though he had mentioned some, but even if he had known, it wouldn't have changed anything. The wad of bills, easily a thousand dollars, spoke to why the road agents had waylaid him. The three would have been rich and a week on the trail before anyone began to worry about why Harris hadn't been seen. He had just started on a buying trip to Denver and likely had told everyone in Taos who cared that he would be gone a couple weeks.

Zamora pressed into the wound. It bubbled blood, but the flow grew increasingly sluggish. He reached for a slender metal probe and gently inserted it into the wound. Slocum heard the dull *click* when the tip touched the buried bullet. Zamora drew back and dropped the bloody probe on the table. Before he could say a word, Harris reached up with a surprisingly strong hand and grabbed the doctor's lapel.

"I can answer what you're thinking, Doctor," Harris said. "I'm dying. I feel it inside. Nothing you or anyone who's not God can do for me."

"I can try to remove the bullet, but . . ." Zamora's words trailed off.

"You just think you're God," Harris said. "You're not." He closed his eyes and arched his back, crying in pain. As the spasm subsided, he opened his eyes again and looked straight at Slocum. "Thanks, John. You've done more for me than I'd expect, even from a best friend."

"You said you had family. I'll go fetch them," Slocum said.

"No, wait, wait. I want to give you something."

Slocum's eyes darted to the money.

"You give that to your family."

"Not that, not for you." Harris's voice faded, then returned a little louder. "As you're my witness, Dr. Zamora, I'm selling the Black Hole to him. To John Slocum. Write up a bill of sale real quick so I can sign."

"You don't have to give me anything," Slocum said.

"You didn't have to fight off them damned 'shiners tryin' to k-k-kill me, either." Harris closed his eyes. For a moment he looked dead, then came back. "Write it up, Doctor. And don't do it with that hen scratching of yours. Write it all neat and proper."

"If you like, Tom."

The doctor quickly went over to a rolltop desk in the corner, pulled out a sheet of stationery from one of the built-in shelves, dipped his pen in the inkwell, and wrote something out.

Slocum watched the life draining from the man. His face turned pale and his eyelids fluttered like tiny bird's wings, but his hand was steady when Zamora put the pen in it. Harris rolled onto his side and affixed his name to the bottom of the paper, which the doctor held steady for him.

He looked up at Zamora and tapped the pen against the bill of sale.

"You witness it."

"To be legal, he has to give you something for it," the doctor said.

"You got a dollar, John?"

Slocum fished a silver dollar from his vest pocket and pressed it into Harris's hand. The man looked at it. A curious smile came to his lips.

"Ought to be pennies for my eyes. That's the way they used to do it. Put pennies on a dead man's eyes."

"You'll make it," Slocum said.

He spoke to a dead man.

2

"He wasn't right in his head," the doctor said.

Slocum looked at the deed in his hand. His thumb rested on a spot of ink and smeared it. Instinctively, he blew on the signature to dry it, to make it permanent, to give him full title to a saloon he had never even seen. Slocum looked up.

"The money belongs to his family. So does this. Where can I find them?"

Dr. Zamora shrugged.

"There's only his sister." The doctor pulled a sheet over Tom Harris and took a deep breath. "I better let the marshal know. Everything that's happened tells me Tom was held up outside town by road agents and that you had nothing to do with the robbery."

"I saved him long enough for him to die here."

Zamora spun and fixed Slocum with a hard stare.

"Nobody could have saved him. The wound was too serious."

"Nobody could have saved him," Slocum repeated slowly, letting it sink into the doctor's head. "I tried. You tried. The three men who tried to rob him killed him. They succeeded where we failed."

"Get out of here. Tom was a good man."

Slocum folded the deed to the Black Hole Saloon and stepped outside into the crisp air and bright high country sunshine. Zamora blamed him for Harris's death, as crazy as that might be. He had no doubt Harris would have died out on the road and had his money stolen, to boot, without any help. By bringing him back to Taos, Slocum had saved that bankroll for his family. For his sister, the doctor had said.

He wandered the winding dirt streets, past markets and through the plaza. He sat and watched the bustle of commerce in the town while he collected his thoughts. When he tired of this, he found a street angling off to the northwest and eventually came on a string of cantinas, one next to another. The Black Hole sat at the end of the street, also a single-story adobe but larger than the rest. Slocum stood in the doorway and inhaled.

Cigar smoke caused his nostrils to dilate. The thick smoke was cut with stale beer and the stench of unwashed patrons. He went into the dimly lit saloon and let his eyes adjust.

He decided this was his kind of place. The woman behind the polished bar was about the prettiest thing he had seen in a month of Sundays. She wore her long brunette hair held back with a turquoise ring. An Indian necklace hung around her neck and fell down between her lush breasts, hidden by a canvas apron drawn up to protect a peasant blouse from myriad spills of beer and whiskey.

Her chocolate eyes fixed on him. She smiled as she came over.

"You knock off some of that trail dust while I fix you up with a drink. Whiskey? Beer?"

"Beer," Slocum said, watching with some appreciation as the woman bent over to draw the beer from a keg behind the bar. He dropped a dime on the bar and quickly got a nickel in change. "I'm looking for Tom Harris's sister."

"Are you now," the woman asked, her eyes narrowing. "Why might that be?"

"My name's John Slocum."

"Annabelle," she said. "So why are you looking for her, John Slocum?"

Slocum took a deep drink and let the beer wash away some of the dust in his throat. He put the mug down on the bar carefully before answering.

"That's personal."

"She doesn't know you."

"You're Harris's sister?"

"You're quick to pick up on that," she said. "Tom's not here right now. I'm running the place for him until he gets back."

"From Denver," Slocum said. He wished he had ordered a shot of whiskey. Or a bottle. It would take more than a beer to make it palatable telling her the unpleasant news.

"How do you know that?"

"Your brother's at Dr. Zamora's. He was ambushed outside town."

"Tom? He's hurt? Oh, *madre de Dios!*" She stripped off the canvas apron and draped it over the bar.

"No, he's not hurt," Slocum said. "He's dead."

She put both hands on the bar to steady herself, then looked at him with a fierceness he hadn't expected.

"I'll cut your heart out with a butter knife if this is a joke." She shoved back, vaulted the bar, and ran out the door, leaving Slocum staring after her.

He started to follow. Zamora could explain as well as he could, but he felt that he hadn't told her of Harris's death properly. Death came suddenly all around him, and sugar-coating the news never occurred to him. He should have eased her into the realization. He turned to go when two men at the far end of the bar called to him.

"You done run her off, mister. You shouldn't have done that."

"No, reckon not," Slocum said.

"We need a couple more beers. You gonna fetch 'em for us or do we have to help ourselves?"

Slocum almost told the cowboy what he could do with the beer, then touched his coat pocket where the deed to the Black Hole Saloon rested. He didn't consider this his saloon but finding himself so engrossed with the Harris family put an obligation on his shoulders. He went around, ducked under the end of the bar, and found two clean mugs, filled them, and dropped the two in front of the cowboys.

"Nickel each," he said.

"Well, now, mister, Annabelle, she's sorta taken a shine to us and lets us run a tab. You just add it to our bill." The one speaking looked at the other and grinned, showing a broken front tooth.

Slocum grabbed the front of the man's shirt and slammed him facedown onto the bar. A second tooth remained embedded in the wood.

"No tabs," he said. "You pay cash or you get out. Your choice."

"No need to get all huffy, mister. Here." The second cowboy counted out ten pennies, which Slocum scooped up with a swipe of his hand. In the same motion he dumped the coins into a ceramic pot under the bar.

"Hey, barkeep, I'll have a shot of rotgut, if you promise it's gonna take the hide off my tongue."

Slocum went to the other end of the bar, snaring a bottle of whiskey as he went. He held it up, swirled it around, and saw milky currents in the amber fluid.

"This tarantula juice'll have you singing songs and thinking you're a maestro," Slocum promised.

"Some of that fer me, too," called another customer.

Slocum got into the job, working from one end to the other, joshing with the customers, badgering others, and enjoying himself despite how he had come to be on this side of the bar. He developed quite a thirst, but rather than drinking the profits, even the paltry amount from a beer, he used a dipper to drink some water from a bucket.

"You know any of them fancy-ass drinks? The ones we hear about from Frisco?"

Slocum poured from one bottle and another, adding a touch of nitric acid he found in a thick glass bottle, and assured the man this was the only thing the railroad barons drank in the Union Club perched stop San Francisco's Nob Hill.

He was fixing a second concoction of his own creation when he saw Annabelle come back in. Her eyes were puffy and red. She had cried herself out from the set to her shoulders, the way she held her chin high, and how she walked with grim determination. Behind her a slender man with thin mustaches waxed to needle points looked around the saloon.

The man wore a gaudy brocade vest and fancy gray trousers with a thin black ribbon running from waist to cuff on the outside of each pant leg. A gold chain dangled from one pocket to another. With hands so delicate as to be effete, he took out a fancy gold watch, popped it open, and studied it as if the secrets of the universe were written on the face. He made a big show of snapping the lid shut, twirled his mustaches to even thinner tips, and came around the bar.

"You are relieved of your duty, sir."

"And you are?" Slocum asked.

"That there's Frenchy Dupont," the customer who had downed Slocum's first potent libation said. His words came out slurred. Slocum had gotten him knee-walking drunk with a single drink.

"My name is Pierre Dupont, if you please."

"Suspect it's Pierre Dupont even if I don't please," Slocum said.

He saw how the thin man's hand moved to his left cuff.

There might be a hideout pistol tucked there, but Slocum guessed a knife sheathed along his forearm was more likely.

"About time for me to tend to other business," Slocum said. He went around the bar and faced Annabelle Harris.

"Dr. Zamora said you saved Tom. Out on the road. When he was attacked." Annabelle looked him squarely in the eye. "Thank you."

"Wish it could have been more."

"It was a great deal. The doctor gave me the money Tom took with him. That will go a long way toward . . . toward keeping the bar in business."

Slocum touched the deed in his pocket, then decided this wasn't the time to deal with what the woman would see as an intrusion. He could sign it over to her later when her grief had faded a mite.

"I have horses with a X Bar X brand. You know of such a ranch in these parts?"

"That's the Deutsch spread out west of town, up in the mountains," Pierre said. "What business do you have with Rory Deutsch?"

"Reckon that's my business—and his," Slocum replied. To Annabelle, he said, "Sorry your brother didn't make it. He was a brave man, holding off three road agents the way he did."

She started to say something but Pierre drew her attention. She smiled weakly, laid her hand on Slocum's shoulder for a moment, then went to tend to business. Slocum saw how Pierre glared at him and considered telling Annabelle then and there that he owned the Black Hole just to fire the Frenchman. She could rehire him when he deeded the bar back to her, but firing Pierre would give him a moment of enjoyment.

Slocum said nothing, however, and stepped outside. The three horses sporting the X Bar X brand tugged nervously at their reins. They were a high-strung lot. Slocum wondered if they took that from their owners. He mounted his

Appaloosa and led the other horses from Taos, heading west across a scary bridge over a deep gorge with the Rio Grande running loud and fast at the bottom. He kept riding until he found the double-rutted road leading into the hills.

With tall mountains all around, the sun disappeared fast in front of him. Slocum camped for the night near a stream, washing off the dirt and enjoying the solitude of the high country. An hour after daybreak, he rode under the wrought iron arch proclaiming this to be the X Bar X.

It took another fifteen minutes before he reached the ranch house. He came to a stop and looked at the fancy two-story dwelling. Deutsch's prosperity showed at every turn, though it seemed on the wane. The barn needed painting and the house, once well kept, now showed need of minor repairs. A couple dozen yards away a goodly-sized bunkhouse might be home to as many as twenty hands.

He stopped his appraisal of Rory Deutsch's wealth when a short, slender man with a rifle came onto the front porch. From the way the rifle pointed in his direction, Slocum knew he hadn't snuck up on anyone.

"What do you want?" the resonant voice boomed forth.

Slocum rode closer, the three horses trailing him. He stopped a decent distance away. The fine etching on the side of the Henry in the man's hands told Slocum this wasn't some rifle grabbed off a gunsmith's rack for knockabout work on the range. Like everything else around here, it was expensive.

"Happened on three horses wearing your brand. Thought you might like to get them back."

The man stepped out into the sun. He kept the rifle aimed in Slocum's direction.

"Where'd you get them?"

Slocum considered what to say.

"Well, now, they were running loose on the far side of Taos. I'm passing through and asked around the pueblo.

A barkeep told me this is your brand. If you're Rory Deutsch, that is."

"Those horses were stolen from my pasture."

"You got them back now."

"How do I know you weren't the one that took them?" Deutsch stepped a little closer and lifted the rifle to his shoulder. The man was weathered like a wrangler's work glove and had the look in his eye of one mean son of a bitch.

"You don't look like a goddamn fool," Slocum said. The man snugged the rifle stock into his shoulder and drew a bead. "Nobody but a goddamn fool would think the man who stole your horses would come all this way to return them."

"You're not getting a reward."

"Never asked for one. Fact is, you don't likely have enough to pay me for my time. It's real valuable, my time." Slocum saw the man's face turn red with anger under the tan. Pushing him much further would cause lead to fly. Slocum sat with his right hand on his saddle horn, but it was only inches from the butt of his Colt. He wore a cross-draw holster for a reason. He could get his pistol out and firing fast without any fumbling.

"Go to hell."

"These *are* your nags?"

"They're mine. The best in northern New Mexico!"

"Won't dispute that," Slocum said, putting enough sarcasm into his tone to suggest he didn't believe it and thought anyone who did was touched in the head. "Good day." Slocum dropped the reins and started to ride away.

"Hold on. Go another foot and I swear I'll shoot you."

Slocum looked back over his shoulder as Deutsch hiked the rifle up to fire.

"Shoot many men in the back?" Slocum goaded him. His fingers curled around the ebony handle of his Colt Navy. With a single move, he could send a round in Deutsch's direction if it looked as if the rancher was going to carry out his threat.

"I want to make sure you didn't steal anything from the saddlebags." Deutsch pawed through the saddlebags and finally stepped away. "Nothing's missing."

Slocum knew what was in them. He had already searched for anything that might identify the three road agents that had killed Tom Harris. All he had found were trail supplies and enough ammunition to start a small war.

"You can get on out of here. Fast." Deutsch waved his rifle.

"You're welcome for me returning those horses." Slocum couldn't help adding, "Mighty strange that you put horses out to pasture all saddled like that, though."

Deutsch roared and fired his rifle in the air. Slocum held his Appaloosa steady with his knees. He had seen the man's anger reach the boiling point and had been ready for the discharge. Taking pleasure in taunting the man had been dangerous, but he had learned a few things. Rory Deutsch was not only an arrogant bastard but also a whale of a liar.

Slocum caught movement in an upstairs window. He shifted to go for his six-shooter, then saw a young woman watching him. Ignoring Deutsch, he tipped his hat to the woman, then rode off. The hair on the back of his neck rose. He couldn't tell if the reaction came from waiting for a rifle bullet to shatter his spine or the pretty woman's hot gaze.

3

Slocum rode with one eye on his back trail. Rory Deutsch hadn't given any hint of hospitality or gratitude at getting his three horses back. Slocum didn't believe for an instant the horses had been stolen, not saddled like they were. Demanding to search the saddlebags to see if Slocum had stolen anything showed that the rancher knew who had ridden those horses. Slocum didn't have to be a betting man to figure that Deutsch himself rode one of them, probably the paint since the road agents on the two chestnuts were larger men.

Slocum kept a *very* sharp eye out for the three ambushers to come after him.

He camped in a cave to reduce the chance that they might see him easily out in the open. The cave was shallow and cold, and he had to build his cooking fire just beyond the mouth, giving away his position to anyone with a sharp eye. He considered the chances of someone sneaking up on him while he slept if he kept the fire for warmth against the mountain chill. His survival instincts told him to pull the blanket up around his shoulders a little more and let the fire die.

Midmorning the next day he rode back into Taos, still aching from the night spent in the mountains. The pueblo with its winding streets lined with adobe buildings offered him a good change, not only from sleeping on the trail but also from the big-city rush of Denver, where he'd just spent some time. He couldn't help thinking of the differences between himself and Tom Harris. Harris had been going to Denver with a wad of greenbacks big enough to choke a cow. Slocum had ridden from that city with only a few dollars in his pocket. Harris had been killed; Slocum had survived. Strangest of all, Harris had owned the Black Hole Saloon and that was now Slocum's. Legally, it was his, but he had done nothing to deserve it and certainly nothing to take it away from Annabelle Harris.

He needed to talk to her, but first he wanted to have words with the marshal about Rory Deutsch and his part in killing Harris. It was spiderweb-thin evidence at best, but anyone who sent out his cowboys to waylay a businessman had to be suspected of other crimes.

The jailhouse looked no different from the other buildings around it. The adobe walls might be three feet thick instead of two and some windows had bars over them. Otherwise, he wouldn't have found it without the sign swinging on a post in front. He dismounted, considered what he expected to learn and if it was worth the risk that the lawman had a poster with his likeness nailed up on a wall, then lashed the reins to a hitching post and went inside.

A smallish man with a full beard and a trapped look snapped alert from cleaning his gun on a battered desk set in the corner.

"You the marshal?"

"Name's Donnelly. What do you want from me?"

Slocum pulled up a chair and sat opposite the man. The marshal's eyes darted around, as if Slocum intended to do him harm and he sought a way to escape.

"You heard about Tom Harris getting himself shot up."

"Poor bastard died. You the one what brought him in to the doc? Zamora gave a good description of you."

Slocum touched the deed in his pocket but decided he was more curious about Deutsch.

"The road agents who killed him rode horses with the X Bar X brand. I took the horses back to Rory Deutsch. He spun some tall tale of how the horses were stolen from his pasture."

"Not my jurisdiction. He's too far out of town fer me to be involved."

"He had the look of a prosperous rancher. Why would he send his men out to rob Harris?"

"You got proof he done that? Take it to the sheriff."

"More interested in hearing about Deutsch. He the kind to skirt the law or maybe even bust a law or two, just to get his way?"

"What rich man don't do that?" Donnelly peered at Slocum. "This ain't any of yer business. Why don't you ride on out and let things be?"

"Tom Harris was an upstanding citizen of Taos, from all I hear. You're not interested in who killed him?"

"Happened out of town, not my jurisdiction. I liked Tom good enough. He stood me a drink or two when I made my nightly rounds. Even my deputies liked him, and they don't like nobody much."

"So—" Slocum was interrupted when the jail door slammed hard against the wall.

A man with a serape slung over his shoulder stood just outside. His sombrero about filled the doorway.

"Marshal, you must come quick. There's a fight."

"Settle down, José. You're all out of breath."

Slocum moved his chair to take in both the lawman and the messenger. José gulped down several deep breaths of the thin air and finally blurted out, "He is going to kill her! Señorita Harris. He waves his knife all around and will cut her!"

"At the saloon?" Marshal Donnelly fumbled to put his six-shooter back together. If his marksmanship was as good as his mechanical skills, Annabelle Harris was doomed.

Slocum pushed to his feet.

"The marshal will be along soon," he said. "Are they at the Black Hole?"

"*Sí*, yes, at the Black Hole."

Slocum mounted and trotted through the dusty streets to the saloon. From the outside, nothing appeared wrong. When he came even with the door, he heard Pierre shouting in French. Slocum didn't have to know the language to understand dire things were happening.

He kicked free of the Appaloosa, dropped to the ground, and stepped just inside the door. The lamps were turned down, turning the interior to twilight. Hand resting on his six-gun but not drawing, Slocum homed in on the shouting.

At the rear of the saloon Pierre waved a wicked long-bladed knife about. The bright shaft reflected the wan light and left silvery trails in the air as he slashed back and forth. He was a menacing figure, but Annabelle Harris seemed no less threatening with a broken whiskey bottle in one hand and a bung starter in the other. Pierre lunged for her. She blocked the thrust with the mallet and viciously swung for his face with the sharp-edged bottle.

"You slut. You have no right to be here."

"I told Tom you were a crook, that he should have sent you packing."

"Both of you, back off," Slocum bellowed.

For a moment, they stared at each other, then realized a third combatant had entered their fray. Slocum aimed his Colt at a spot between them. The threat was obvious. If either crossed his line of fire, they'd catch a bullet.

"This is not your fight," Pierre said. "Leave now."

"He thinks he owns the Black Hole because Tom's dead. He's wrong."

"I worked for pennies. He owed me. I claim the bar for my own!"

Slocum fired as Pierre surged forward. The bullet missed the Frenchman's hand but tore away part of his left sleeve, revealing the sheath along his forearm.

"Damn," Slocum said. "I'm usually a better shot. Next one goes through your heart."

"Kill him!" raged Annabelle. "Go on, shoot him down! He deserves it, trying to steal Tom's property. *My* property now."

Slocum fired again as both of them stepped forward to renew their fight.

"What's going on here?" Marshal Donnelly crept in, a shotgun in his trembling hands. Slocum saw that the lawman wasn't wearing his six-shooter. It probably had been too much of a chore to reassemble it, and it must still have lain in pieces on his desk.

"This is a private squabble, Marshal," Pierre said. "I own the Black Hole, and she tried to kill me."

"My bother died! I'm his only kin. The Black Hole is all I've got!"

Slocum fired again as Pierre and Annabelle squared off to renew the fight. He ignored the marshal and his shotgun. The flustered lawman might have left his office in such a rush that he hadn't bothered to load the gun.

"Turns out, you're both wrong," Slocum said. "I'm the owner. Tom signed it over to me before he died."

Silence fell on the saloon so intense it almost hurt Slocum's ears. Finally, all three of the others spoke at once.

"No, it is not possible."

"He wouldn't!"

"Who're you to be—"

Slocum fired again. He was quickly approaching the point where he needed to settle this dispute peaceably or reload for a real fight.

"Everyone settle down. Harris signed over the saloon to

me on his deathbed, and Dr. Zamora witnessed it." He pulled the deed from his pocket and held it out for the marshal.

The man took the sheet as if it would burn his fingers. He squinted and sucked on his teeth and finally said, "Looks all signed and proper to me."

"It's a forgery!" Annabelle blurted out. "Tom would never give the Black Hole to a stranger!"

"It is mine by right. I worked for nothing because he promised me the deed when he died." Pierre puffed himself up and crossed his arms.

"He did no such thing," Annabelle said, angrily facing Pierre. "I never liked you. I don't know why Tom kept you around since you were stealing from him! From me and him!"

"Hush up, everyone. I'll take this over to the doc and see if he can back up the claim." Donnelly peered closer at the paper, then up. "You're this here John Slocum named in the deed?"

"Better get to it, Marshal," Slocum said.

"I'm coming with you," Annabelle said.

"I, too, will accompany you to end this farce!" Pierre tucked his knife back into the forearm sheath. From the way his right hand twitched, he wanted to use it on Annabelle.

For her part, she put down the broken bottle and then tossed the bung starter on top of it. The trio stormed from the saloon, leaving Slocum alone. He holstered his six-gun, found a broom, and began cleaning up. It wouldn't do to have his watering hole all dirty.

After a couple hours behind the bar, Slocum began to tire of the constant din and requests for more beer, more whiskey, more fancy drinks. He had found a bartender's guide with recipes for the outrageously named drinks, but ignoring the proportions proved a hit with the customers. They didn't want strange, new flavors. They wanted alcohol to get drunk.

Slocum furnished floods of it, but being a solitary creature, he was finally worn down by the constant demands on his attention. What didn't bother him at all was the overflowing ceramic pot stuffed with money. Half was greenbacks that might not be worth using to light a quirrly, but the coins jingled and clanked nicely as he dropped them in. Several of the cowboys and vaqueros paid with gold coins. These he slipped into his vest pocket because it felt good having money again after so long. Best of all, he didn't have to rob anyone to get rich. The customers almost forced the money on him.

That eased his discomfort at having so many crowded into the small saloon.

But as the evening wore on, he realized he had to sign the business over to Annabelle. He had earned it by fighting off the road agents, at least in Tom Harris's eyes. As he set up more beer mugs and wiped clean the used ones, he wondered if he could get Annabelle to take him on as a partner. She was a mighty pretty filly, but he had seen how her temper flared. Pierre hadn't deterred her with his knife. She had stood up to him and given as good as she got.

Such a feisty woman would be a handful. Slocum let his mind drift as he mindlessly swabbed off the bar and took money in exchange for the beer. Having her beside him as a partner—maybe even a bed partner—appealed to him. He knew nothing about the nuts and bolts of running a business. Right now, he served liquor already stored in the back room. Harris had been on his way to Denver to buy more.

Slocum had no idea what made a good deal buying booze.

"You backstabbin', no-account cheat!"

The insult rang out over the din in the Black Hole and drew Slocum's attention to a table at the rear where five men played poker. He had considered putting in a faro table but there was little enough room. He knew tonight's crowd would fade over the weeks. Right now everyone flocked in to see the new owner. It would take games like faro with a pretty dealer or waitresses showing a bit of ankle and breast to keep the crowds coming back.

He shook himself. He was planning for a future he didn't want to live in.

Slocum vaulted the bar and took four quick steps through the crowd, pushing men away in time to grab a gambler's wrist as he drew a derringer. A quick turn twisted the man's arm back at an unnatural angle, forcing him to drop the hideout gun.

"No gunplay, not in my place," Slocum said. Over the years he had worked as a bouncer in even rowdier saloons. Quelling the fight fast made sense. If it got out of hand, everyone would be trading punches and would wreck the place. "What's the trouble?"

"He had three aces!" The cowboy across the table was so close to passing out, he hardly focused his eyes. Slocum looked closer and saw one eye wandered off all by its lonesome. The dozen shots of whiskey hadn't done anything to keep it in the corral.

"So? That's a winning hand," grumbled the gambler as he rubbed his wrist where Slocum had wrenched it around.

"Two of 'em was spades! Ain't no honest deck that has two aces of spades in it!"

Slocum slammed his hand onto the cards in front of the gambler to keep him from scooping them up. He flipped them over, then looked up.

"You're wrong," he told the cowboy. "There aren't two aces of spades."

"But—" the man protested, turning his head so the wandering eye could better see the cards spread out on the table.

"There's three." Slocum grabbed the gambler by the collar and lifted him bodily. "No cheating in the Black Hole."

Slocum heaved him out into the street. The gambler sat and reached for a vest pocket. Slocum cleared leather and fired before the tinhorn pulled out a second derringer. The slug ripped into the man's right shoulder and knocked him flat onto his back.

"Next shot will be through your heart, though I might

not be a good enough shot to find something that small and rotten." Slocum saw comprehension dawn on the gambler's face that he had just committed an act that should have ended his life.

He rolled to hands and knees, clumsily stood, and ran away, clutching his injured shoulder. Slocum picked up the derringer and tucked it into his coat pocket next to the saloon deed Donnelly had returned hours earlier. Heaving a sigh, he went back into the smoky room. For a moment, silence descended, then a roar went up and Slocum found a dozen patrons slapping him on the back and wishing him well.

"Nope, not going to do it," he said once he had returned to his post behind the bar. "You all got to pay for your own drinks."

"Ah, Slocum, you're a spoilsport."

"If there's going to be drinks on the house, it'll be on *your* house," he told the patron.

This caused a roar of laughter at the man's expense, but he took it well. Slocum slipped him a free beer, put his finger to his lips, then went on collecting another small fortune as he sold drinks along the entire length of the bar.

The crowd began to peter out around midnight, and Slocum saw he had to restock the backbar's whiskey. He knew something of mixing up trade whiskey, but figured he would have turned the saloon back to Annabelle before he had to pour the raw alcohol, gunpowder, rusty nails, and all the rest into a vat to make more. When his last two customers snored peacefully at tables, heads on crossed arms, he went to the storeroom to replenish his stock.

He cursed under his breath. A padlock secured the door to keep customers from sneaking back there and drinking themselves into a stupor for free. Harris had signed the deed over; he hadn't told Slocum any of the details of running the business such as where the key might be found. Slocum looked in the obvious places behind the bar, then returned and checked the door frame for a hole where a key might be hidden.

As his fingers moved across the lintel, finding only dirt, he froze. Sounds from the storeroom warned him someone was moving about there. He knew better than to shoot off a lock. The ricochet was as likely to hit him as it was to break the lock. He drew his pistol and slammed the butt into the top of the lock. It yielded with a loud snap.

He tossed the broken lock away, lifted the latch, and kicked open the door.

"Hands up!" He stepped in, six-gun trained on a man tearing off the top of a crate and smashing the bottles of whiskey against the floor.

Distracted by counting the bottles already shattered, Slocum failed to see there were two men in the room. Apparently they had broken in through the back entrance, which Slocum realized when he looked up and noticed a rear door that was half open. The second man swung a broom against his wrist hard enough to make Slocum's grip go limp. He dropped his six-shooter. Then he was enfolded by strong arms and driven into the wall. He recoiled and brought his knee up to crush his attacker's groin.

The man grunted. The steel grip around Slocum's arms weakened. Slocum jerked around and sent the man stumbling into his partner. They went down in a welter of elbows and assholes amid the broken glass and puddles of pungent whiskey.

Slocum reached for his fallen gun but slipped in the whiskey. This was all it took for one man to heave a broken bottle at him. The sharp edge cut his forehead. The rush of blood momentarily blinded Slocum, but his fingers wrapped around the butt of his Colt. He squeezed off a round, not caring where the slug went. Creating confusion gave him time enough to swipe at the blood blinding him.

Through the black curtain caused by the blood in his eyes, he saw the men going for their six-shooters. He fired again but a third time the hammer fell on a spent round.

Slocum cursed his bad luck. He had forgotten to reload after stopping the fight between Annabelle and Pierre.

"Nobody beats on me and lives to brag on it," growled an intruder. He raised his gun.

The report filled Slocum's ears and deafened him. He kept wiping at the blood and cleared his vision. A sudden gust of cold air hit him in the face at the same instant another gunshot rang out, this one inches from his ear. He flinched away and turned to see Annabelle Harris standing over him, holding a six-gun in both hands.

"Thanks," he said. "You scared them off." A gust of wind slammed the back door as the two men fled.

Slocum sat straighter when he saw the look on her face. She stepped away, cocked the thumb buster, and pointed it straight at him.

"Missed them. Won't miss you," she said.

The bore looked as big as a train tunnel—and it didn't tremble with the least bit of hesitation on the determined woman's part as she curled her finger around the trigger.

4

"I want the deed. Tear it up," Annabelle Harris said. "Do it now or I'll shoot you."

Slocum reached into his coat pocket and touched the derringer he had taken from the gambler. It would be a difficult shot, squeezing off a round and firing through his coat. He turned slightly, squeezed the trigger to distract her, and launched himself across the floor. The slick whiskey kept him sailing along. The broken glass slashed at his arm and side, but he crashed into the woman, hitting her just under the knees.

She let out a yelp and threw up her hands in a reaction she couldn't have avoided. It came second nature to anyone falling backward. Her six-gun went flying and hit the wall. When it discharged, she cried out again. But this time, she found herself pinned to the floor, Slocum's knees pressing into her shoulders in a schoolboy pin. Struggle as she might, she couldn't budge his greater weight.

"Settle down," he said. Slocum had to smile. How often had he said that in the past twelve hours? It always came with Annabelle in some fight. "I'm not going to keep the saloon."

"What? Why not? You rooked Tom out of it."

"Did you talk to Dr. Zamora?"

"You paid him off to lie. You must have!"

"I never met Zamora before. Is he the kind of man to be bought off so easily?"

"Easily? You could have given him hundreds of dollars as a bribe. Who knows what a poor doctor's price is?"

"Why bother returning the thousand that your brother had on him? I could have ridden away with his money and the three horses I took from the road agents."

"Nobody said anything about horses." She stopped fighting him.

He stared down into her lovely face. Her hair sprayed out around her head, soaking up whiskey. Rocking back, he took some pressure off her shoulders to test what she would do. When he saw the resignation on her face, he knew the fight was gone out of her. He let her up.

He stood, then helped her to her feet.

"I've got booze in my hair. I smell like a distillery," she said, trying to squeeze out the potent liquor. She cried out when she cut her fingers on glass stuck in her hair.

"Be careful. There're shards all over." Slocum winced and clutched his side. For the first time he realized how badly cut up he had gotten rolling around on the floor.

"You're bleeding. From that cut on your forehead but also through your coat." Annabelle reached out. Now her hand shook as she peeled away the coat and tugged at his vest.

"Doesn't feel too bad. My clothes took a worse beating than I did." Slocum stretched. "Only shallow cuts."

"Come along," she said in a tone that demanded obedience. When he stared at her, she said, "I used to be a schoolteacher. Now come along."

"If I don't, will you make me stand in the corner?"

This brought bright laughter to her lips.

"You might wish for such minor punishment," she said.

"I was quite good with a willow switch." She snared his hand and pulled him along to the bar.

The two drunks were gone and the front door had been locked. She had closed up and then followed him into the back room.

"You pulled my bacon out of the fire."

"I saved your life. Admit it," she said as she tugged on his coat and got him out of it before starting to unbutton his vest.

"You did that very thing," Slocum allowed.

This took her by surprise.

"You're not arguing the point?"

"No reason. It's true."

"You aren't anything like I thought," she said. "Turn around. I can't get your shirt off with you standing there facing me."

As he turned, she unstuck the cloth from the wound. He had been right. Only a scratch but it bled enough to make it look worse than it was. He cried out, then bit his lip when a sudden rush of liquor over the wound burned like fire.

"A couple pieces of glass are still in the wound. Don't move."

He sucked in a breath and held it as she fished out the glass with the tip of a knife she took from under the bar. The slivers made tinkling sounds as they dropped to the floor. A second splash of whiskey stung, but not as bad this time.

"Doesn't even need stitches." She stepped back and studied him critically. Then she looked up at him, opened her mouth, and started to say something but bit back the words.

"What were you going to say?" he asked, turning to her.

Her voice was small and almost too low for him to hear.

"I was going to ask if you wanted me to kiss it and make it well."

"No need to get those lovely lips of yours all bloody." He

stepped closer and pulled her to him. She resisted, hands pressing into his bare chest. Slocum held her to keep her from escaping but did nothing to pull her closer. He felt her resistance melting away like snow in a warm spring sun.

She eased closer, then passionately kissed him. It was as if a dam broke. One instant, drought. The next, a flood.

She pressed hard against him. He felt the crush of her breasts hidden behind her peasant blouse. The turquoise necklace and her bracelets cut into him. He never noticed because of the intoxicating taste of her lips. When his lips parted slightly, she boldly thrust her tongue into his mouth. All shyness vanished as she hungrily kissed him.

Their tongues darted back and forth, stroking, caressing, driving like fleshy battering rams. They ebbed and flowed, changing the manner of the kiss until both had to break off and gasp for breath.

She looked at him, eyes wide in wonder.

"I want you so," she said. "I don't know why, but I do. I need you."

Her hands fumbled and freed him of his gun belt, then worked on the buttons on his fly. As she popped them open one by one, he occupied himself sliding his hands under her blouse, then lifting. For a moment, they worked at odds, then she stopped her quest for the hardness sprouting from his crotch to raise her arms high over her head. The blouse slipped free, leaving her as bare to the waist as he was.

The necklace dangled now between her bare breasts.

"Your skin is so white and smooth," he said, running his fingers over the sleek cones, "and the blue stones make them stand out."

He pressed his thumbs into the taut pink nipples until she closed her eyes and sighed in pleasure. He released them and rubbed the turquoise over her flesh. This excited her even more, the feel of slick cool stone contrasting with the warmth of his fingers.

"I do, I do want you, John," she said.

Annabelle backed away, then reached behind, caught the edge of the bar, and hopped up. She rocked back, lifted her ass, and scooted her skirt up around her waist to expose her bare pubes.

He bent forward and licked at the cleft. She cried out as he continued to lave the pinkly scalloped nether lips. When he thrust his tongue into her hot center, she collapsed onto the bar.

Slocum was so hard now that he hurt. He finished the chore of opening his fly and slid his arms under her knees. A quick pull flattened Annabelle on the bar and drew her closer to the edge. Slocum bent her double by hiking her knees over his shoulders and leaned forward. The tip of his manhood lightly dragged along her trembling privates.

"Don't tease, John. Do it. I want you inside me!"

He ignored her. He slid up and down, getting her inner oils all over his length as he worked her to a fever pitch. She thrashed about, but he held her securely and controlled her by keeping those two long legs over his shoulders. When he couldn't stand it any longer, he leaned forward and thrust with his hips.

The bulbous tip missed and skittered along her cleft again. She moaned and protested. Then she shrieked in delight as he moved into her with a smooth, long shove. For an instant he was transported to a different world, one of stark pleasure and complete lust.

She tensed around him as he began to pull free. When only the plum-shaped tip of his dick remained in her, he paused, caught his breath, and then slowly reentered. She went wild with desire. He found the slow movements difficult to maintain. His own ardor threatened to cause him to erupt at any instant. Faster and faster he pistoned into her heated core, liquid squishing sounds drowned out by Annabelle's shrieks of desire.

Her legs clamped hard on his ears as she got off. He arched his back and tried to split her in half with his fleshy sword. Then he exploded. His hips flew like a shuttlecock, and he went limp far too soon.

Sweat poured down his bare chest. He backed away and released his hold on her legs. She flopped weakly, her slender legs on either side of his hips. Her chest heaved and her tits bounced about until she caught her breath. She pushed up to her elbows and looked at him.

"I never imagined," she whispered.

"It can be that way after a close scrape."

"Scrape? Oh, back in the storeroom," Annabelle said, shrugging delightfully. Slocum fought to keep his attention on what she said rather than how her body responded now. "That happens now and again."

"Men smashing your whiskey?"

"Drifters stealing what they can. They—" She bit off the rest of the sentence. Annabelle swallowed hard and finally said, "They weren't stealing the booze. They were destroying it."

"Why'd anyone do that?"

She sat up and wiggled a bit to get her skirts down around her legs. She was still naked to the waist. She shivered and gooseflesh appeared to mar her smooth skin. Putting her hands on his shoulders for balance, she hopped down, bent, and retrieved her blouse. As much as he hated to do so, Slocum knew he had to get dressed, too.

As she pulled the blouse back down over her head, she mumbled to herself. When she was decent again, Annabelle said, "Tom worried about something before he left for Denver."

"Why go all the way north to buy whiskey? Couldn't he buy it here? How hard is it to distill alcohol and then spruce it up?"

"Tom always liked to give the customers a choice between rotgut that would rip out their throats and good stuff from Tennessee and Kentucky. He used to buy it from whiskey peddlers, but they stopped coming by a few months ago."

"Why?"

"I can't say. Tom always took care of supplies."

"And hiring?"

"I never liked Pierre, but Tom insisted on keeping him. He's a good barkeep, but he always treated me with contempt."

"His loss," said Slocum. "You need to be treated in an entirely different way." He ran his fingers through the hair at the back of her head and pulled her close for a quick kiss.

"Oh my, yes, his loss." A shy smile danced on her lips. "My gain."

"You have enough stock to keep the bar going, even after a couple cases of whiskey were broken?"

"I need to see what was damaged. But why would anyone bust it up when they could steal it?"

They returned to the back room. Annabelle lit a kerosene lamp and started to move closer to the stacks of boxes when Slocum held her back.

"The fumes might cause the whole saloon to go up if they catch fire." He went to the rear door, saw how it had been pried open. The crowbar they used lay in the dirt where it had been discarded. He used the crowbar to prop open the door to air out the storeroom.

He looked around the alley but finding the men would be impossible. They'd had plenty of time to hightail it. Stepping back in caused glass to crunch under his boots. Annabelle already swept the broken bottles toward the door to clean up but missed the smaller shards.

"A couple cases are damaged. You must have caught them just as they started."

"You say the whiskey peddlers you used to buy from stopped coming to town a few months back?"

"I heard Pete from over at the Santa Fe Drinking Emporium complain about running low, but that was weeks ago."

"Did he close up?"

"No," she said. "He has plenty of liquor. Wonder where

SLOCUM AND THE THREE FUGITIVES   39

he gets it. I can't see him riding to Denver to buy from dealers there."

"Would his saloon still be open?"

"He runs all night long and only closes up at dawn. Why?"

"I have a couple questions to ask."

"I'll close up," she said, walking over to the back door, removing the crowbar, and slamming the door shut.

Slocum waited for her to leave the storeroom then secured the inner door the best he could without a lock, and returned to the main room. Walking past Annabelle, he went out into the street in front of the Black Hole. She joined him in a minute, carefully locking the front door.

Annabelle grinned. "I still have the keys. Unless you want to take them." She smiled coyly and dropped the keys down her blouse between her breasts.

"I'll hunt for the keys later," Slocum said. His mind wandered to other things.

Annabelle cupped her breasts and bounced them. A tinkling sounded as the keys bounced against her silver and turquoise necklace.

"Sure you don't want to carry the keys?"

"Where's Pete's bar?"

"We can open a case of the best whiskey left. Tom had a good palate for buying bourbon. There's even a decent bottle of brandy that's hardly been touched behind the bar."

He took her by the elbow and steered her toward the town plaza. Annabelle sighed, hung on his arm, and laid her head against his shoulder as they walked.

"He hasn't closed yet," she said, pointing across the plaza to an adobe with an open door and light spilling out. "Won't be long, though. It's almost dawn."

Slocum walked faster when he saw a man struggling to pull the door shut.

"Pete, wait a second," Annabelle called.

"*Hola*, Miss Harris," the man said. "Sorry to hear about your brother."

"Thanks. You closing?"

"Got a couple customers left to toss out. It's been a busy night, and I'm all tuckered out."

"If you'd answer a question, I'd appreciate it," Slocum said. "Miss Harris would appreciate it."

The man glanced from Slocum to the woman. He almost leered when he said, "How appreciative would you be, Annabelle?"

"Not *that* grateful, Pete, you old horny toad." She laughed, letting Slocum know this banter had gone on between her and the other saloon owner before.

"You having supply problems for your whiskey?" Slocum asked. He stood a little straighter when he saw the man's reaction. Even in the dark, he saw the man turn pale. ⚊

"No."

The curt answer only spurred Slocum's curiosity.

"Annabelle said the whiskey peddlers stopped coming to town a few months back. Tom was on his way to Denver to buy his liquor. How are you supplying the booze for your customers?"

Pete stepped out and blocked their entry into the saloon. This put Slocum on his guard. He and Annabelle hadn't made a move to go inside. Pete even glanced over his shoulder as if someone crept up on him to listen to his answer.

"Tom was a hardheaded son of a buck, no offense, Annabelle. He wouldn't knuckle under to no man. Me, I seen enough trouble fighting the Navajo and Ute back in the day. I don't look for trouble."

"What if it hunts you down?" Slocum asked. He separated himself a little from Annabelle so Pete had to turn slightly to look squarely at whichever of them was speaking.

"A man learns how to duck and dodge the older he gets."

"Oh, Pete, you're not that old," Annabelle said. She reached out and took the man's arm, forcing him to look her way.

Slocum caught a quick glance into the saloon and two men sitting near the door. They had a bottle on the table in front of them, but both nursed empty shot glasses. He had seen men intent on eavesdropping. Both of them worried more about what Pete said than filling their own glasses for one last drink.

"You running the Black Hole now, Annabelle, you'll find out what Tom already knew. Or you letting Pierre take charge?"

"If Pierre comes looking for work, think it over carefully before you hire him," Annabelle said angrily.

Pete looked back at Slocum and said, "He your new barkeep?"

"The new owner," Slocum said, to see what reaction this caused.

"Do tell. Didn't take you long to find a buyer." Pete started to look over his shoulder at the two men, then forced himself to remain facing outward. "You'll find supply routes are different in Taos."

"How different?"

"You'll find out. I got to close. Again, Annabelle, sorry about Tom. Damned shame him getting thrown from his horse and dying like that."

Before either Slocum or Annabelle could correct him, Pete ducked into his saloon. The door grated shut and a locking bar fell inside.

"Who were the men in the bar?" Slocum asked.

"They never moved so I didn't get a good look at them. Why?"

Slocum said nothing more. He hadn't seen their faces either, but their clothing was heavily stained. As if they had spilled a lot of whiskey on their coats and pants.

"Do you have a place to stay, John?"

"No. I figured there must be a hotel or boardinghouse."

"I . . . I have a big enough bed for the two of us."

"That's the second best offer I've had all night," he said.

"Second? What? Oh my, John, you are such a joker."

Slocum led her to the plaza and the gazebo in the center. They sat so he could kiss her, hidden by shadows.

"This is nice, but my bed is much more private," Annabelle said.

Slocum waited a few seconds longer until two men rode past, heading away. He craned his neck to get a better look at them, but they wore their hats low and had pulled up bandannas to cover their face against trail dust.

"Lead on," he said. He hardly listened to everything Annabelle said as they walked to a small adobe house on the outskirts of town because he kept turning over everything that had happened.

And that the men who had smashed up the Black Hole whiskey likely had ridden from town on horses with X Bar X brands.

5

Slocum dropped the clawhammer on the bar with a loud bang. Annabelle looked up from the table where she was working on the saloon's books.

"All fixed?" she asked.

"Nobody's getting in the rear door without coming through the wall, and it's two feet thick," Slocum said. He drew himself a beer, downed it, then drew another.

She looked at him in disdain.

He carefully drank another half mug before asking, "You want one?"

"Drinking up the profits is not helping. Water is perfectly good to quench your thirst."

"Beer tastes better," he said, finishing the second mug. He dipped it into the water bucket and it came out brimming with water.

He rounded the bar and sat beside her, looking at the columns of figures.

"You want me to explain these to you?"

"I know how to cipher," he said. "We made a decent profit this past week. Must be the new owner."

"Or his attentive assistant keeping track of how much liquor goes out in every shot and keeping the beer just cool enough so it'll foam just right and fill the mug but not make the customer think he's being cheated."

"We could use a piano player," Slocum said. "Might bring in more customers."

"Not likely we could cover the expense of the piano, the musician, and however much he would steal from us. Any dollar that goes into the piano player's pocket doesn't come to ours."

"What about a faro table? You'd look mighty fine dealing faro," he said, catching the joking tone to her voice. "You'd only have to bend forward a mite—just like you're doing now—and show off those fine teats of yours. Gamblers would completely forget the odds."

"The odds of me doing that are zero," she said.

"What are my odds with you?"

"One hundred percent," Annabelle said, bending over to flash more of her fine breasts as she kissed him.

"I'll sign over the Black Hole to you anytime you want," Slocum said. "You and your brother built this place. I just happened along at a bad time for him and a good one for me."

"No need. Our partnership is working out fine," she said.

"So far. One of these days you're going to kick me out. It'd be to your benefit if you owned the saloon outright."

"You mean you're getting tired of being tied down so long and want to drift on?"

Slocum laughed, but the sound rang hollow in his ears. There was a touch of truth in what Annabelle said. Just a touch. He enjoyed her company, both in bed and out. Just seeing her made him think about settling down. Running a saloon wasn't a bad way to make a living. He had found the more he worked there, both behind the bar and out among the patrons, the less he drank. Part of it was that he no longer needed the liquor to dull the pain of spending long lonely hours on the trail. Another was that he needed his wits sharp and now the beer dulled them.

Putting down roots in Taos was not something he had considered, but he was increasingly amenable to the notion. The people in the pueblo were decent, and Annabelle was enough to make any man forget about riding to the horizon just to see what lay beyond. It wasn't always necessary to ride past the sunset if he shared it with a willing woman as lovely as Annabelle Harris.

"This is a different life for me. I grew up working a farm. The war changed the way I lived."

"You shouldn't feel guilty that you survived and others around you didn't," she said.

"I don't feel guilty. I barely survived."

Unconsciously, his hand pressed into his belly, where Bloody Bill Anderson had gut-shot him after William Quantrill had taken offense. Slocum had said powerful things to Quantrill about how he had ordered his guerrillas to kill every male in Lawrence, Kansas, over the age of eight. Slocum was sure some under that young age had been gunned down just to feed the rebel leader's anger at losing his sister in a federal prison.

It had taken Slocum months to recover. He felt no guilt about the struggle that he'd won and that so many others had lost. A small smile curled his lips. He had heard Quantrill had been killed and his skull sent back to Ohio, where it had been lost. He had kept his head; Quantrill hadn't.

No guilt about that at all.

"We are making money," she said, turning back to the ledger, "but we need to restock. Our whiskey supply is distressingly low."

"That's why Tom was heading up to Denver, to get new shipments."

She nodded somberly.

"What happened to the whiskey peddlers? A town like

Taos ought to have them fighting their way through Raton Pass to supply you."

"I don't know. As I said, Tom always handled that part of the business. I was more a numbers wrangler. This and tending bar." She thumped the ledger.

"You hear anything about Pierre?" he asked suddenly. "He thought he was entitled to the money. Nobody walks away from a pie when he expects to get at least one piece."

"I haven't heard anything more of him. I think he left town," she said.

Slocum doubted that. The former barkeep had been too furious to ride off and not look back. He decided he needed to track the man down and settle the score before considering other saloon business. He downed his water and started to stand when a half-dozen men came in. Slocum sank back into the chair and reached across for the gun butt hanging on his left side.

"You're a dead man if you throw down, Slocum." The owlhoot gestured to the men flanking him. Both leveled shotguns. "I'm Lucas Deutsch and this is my little brother, Timothy."

"Little brother" meant the same as calling a fat man "Skinny." Timothy Deutsch's hat brushed the ceiling. His shoulders were the span of a bull's horns. He opened and closed hands the size of quart jars, as if fantasizing about wrapping them around someone's neck and squeezing out the life.

Slocum's sharp eyes picked out the liquor stains on Lucas Deutsch's vest, a silent testimony to his sloppiness in breaking bottles in the Black Hole's back room a week ago. Which of the other men had been with Deutsch hardly mattered. It hadn't been his "little" brother. Slocum would have identified a hulking giant like him in a flash.

He scowled, pursed his lips, then asked, "I've seen you boys before, haven't I? On the road to Denver?" From the way Timothy Deutsch surged forward, he knew he had hit a nerve.

Slocum gauged his distance and the attack perfectly. He shoved out his foot, caught Deutsch's boot toe, causing him to stumble. Moving fast, Slocum slammed his fist into the back of Timothy Deutsch's skull, stunning him. He knocked away the ten-gallon hat, grabbed the man's greasy hair, and pulled straight back so his throat was taut.

"Kill him," Lucas Deutsch snapped to his henchmen.

"Do that and your brother's blood will make a mighty big puddle on the floor."

Slocum shifted his weight but kept his knee in the center of Deutsch's broad back to show that he had a knife blade pressed against his windpipe.

Lucas Deutsch waved off his gunmen. He stepped around, hand resting on the six-shooter he carried slung low on his hip. Some men merely pretended to be shootists. Slocum saw nothing in this Deutsch's behavior to make him think any part of it was a bluff. The butt of his six-gun was well worn. From what Slocum could see, the pistol was well tended so it wouldn't fail when Deutsch needed it most.

"Don't cut his throat. If you do, she'll be the first to catch a pound of lead." Lucas Deutsch pointed to Annabelle.

"Go to hell," she flared. "I'll—"

"Quiet, Annabelle," Slocum said. "Lower the guns and I won't spray his blood on my nice clean floor."

For some reason Deutsch found this funny. He laughed until tears came to his eyes. He wiped them away with his bandanna, then ordered his men outside.

Only when they had left the saloon did Slocum let the giant off the floor. Timothy Deutsch growled like an animal and started to grab Slocum with his bare hands.

"Heel, boy. We got business. Go outside with the others."

"Luke, I—"

"Do it."

There wasn't any question as to which of the Deutsch brothers called the shots. Timothy lumbered out, ducking to keep from banging his head on the low doorway.

"You just made yourself a terrible enemy," Lucas Deutsch warned.

"Don't care. The bigger they are, the harder they fall."

"Timothy? I didn't mean him. I meant *me*. You made me look dumb in front of my boys. I need to do something to get back my good name." Deutsch hooked a toe around a chair leg and pulled it around, where he could sit facing Slocum and Annabelle. "I was going to offer you all the whiskey you wanted at ten dollars a bottle, but now I can't do that. I do that and the boys think I'm going soft."

"Ten dollars?" Annabelle cried. "Even shipping it from Denver, we wouldn't pay five!" She half stood, then saw Slocum shaking his head, and subsided with ill grace.

He sat beside her as much to keep her in check as to watch Deutsch's reactions. He dropped his knife on the table. It clattered and then silence filled the saloon. Outside Deutsch's men laughed and joked. A team in the street clattered by. From the sound it made, a wheel was close to falling off. Children played a game but soon quieted, probably because of the small gang outside the saloon door.

Inside the Black Hole, the silence became oppressive. Slocum waited. Deutsch had to fill it with words. When he did, they would be more honest than anything he'd said so far.

"Nobody in Taos buys whiskey that's not distilled by the Deutsch family," he said.

"You stopped the whiskey peddlers from coming!" Annabelle sounded outraged.

"A month back. The last one met an unfortunate accident trying to sneak into New Mexico Territory over La Veta Pass." Deutsch shook his head in mock sadness. "Wagon, team, and driver toppled over a cliff. Must have fallen five hundred feet. Never heard such pitiful cries in all my life. All the way down."

"From the team?" Annabelle asked in a low voice.

"From the damned fool whiskey peddler who thought he could cut into my market. You buy at twenty dollars a bottle or you don't buy at all." Deutsch stood so quickly the chair crashed to the floor. "How much you want? We call it Taos Lightning because it's got that kind of a kick."

"We can't afford that much!" Annabelle looked at Slocum, fire in her eyes.

"If you'd played nice, I'd've sold it to you for ten."

"You better leave before you regret it," Slocum said. He fought to keep his own anger in check.

Deutsch laughed harshly, then followed his brother and the rest into the bright afternoon sun. The sound of their boots faded until only normal noises came through the door.

"Tom never told me. That's why he went to Denver."

"The horses I took from the road agents all had X Bar X brands. The Deutsch family controlling all the whiskey in town explains why Rory Deutsch was all upset over seeing the horses. He thought his boys had been killed."

Slocum thought on this. Lucas Deutsch had been one of those waylaying Tom Harris, but the identity of the other two was up in the air. He had been at a distance. One could have been the giant Timothy Deutsch. The other he had the distinct impression of being smaller, small like Rory Deutsch himself, but he could have compared that man with the giant and assumed no one was possibly so big.

"How many sons does Rory Deutsch have?"

Annabelle said, "I don't know. Word was they were on the trail and only got back a month or two ago."

"About the time the whiskey drought hit town," Slocum said. "The boys came home and immediately went into business other than raising cattle."

"We can't afford that much for a bottle, John. We get thirty-five shots from a bottle and charge a dime. We're making three-fifty and paying twenty for a bottle? We'd lose sixteen-fifty for every bottle we sold!"

"Can't see cowboys forking over sixty cents for a shot of whiskey, even if it is good. You ever hear of this Taos Lighting before?" He saw she hadn't. "We need to talk with other owners."

"To unite! We all present a unified front to the Deutsches and we can get our business back to normal!"

Slocum wasn't sure what normal meant, but Annabelle had the right idea.

They closed up the saloon and went to talk with the owner of the Santa Fe Drinking Emporium. Pete sat out front, feet propped up on a nail keg, noisily napping in the sun. It was about siesta time, but Slocum would disturb the sleep of the dead to get back at the Deutsch family. He knew in his gut Lucas and his gang had killed Tom Harris and then tried to extort money from his sister. Nothing about that set well with Slocum.

"Pete, wake up, you lazy bones," Annabelle said, shaking the man's shoulder. He snorted, started, and pushed his hat up to see who'd interrupted his sleep.

"I musta died and gone straight to Heaven 'cuz I'm seein' an angel. Ain't nobody else who'd disturb my siesta."

"Lucas Deutsch and his brother just came by to sell me— us—whiskey at an exorbitant price."

Slocum watched how Pete reacted to Annabelle's news. Earlier she had accused him of feeling guilty about living through the war when so many others hadn't. If she wanted a display of guilt on a man's face, she need only look at Pete. He couldn't even meet her gaze.

"Doin' that to all of us."

"You buy that Taos Lightning from him?" Slocum asked.

"Real fiery shit, that stuff. Liquid death." Even as he said it, he looked around as if he might have been overheard. "Not that. Nobody'd die from it."

"Who's died drinking it? The Taos Lightning?" Slocum demanded.

"Rumors, that's all. Not more 'n a dozen folks," Pete said reluctantly when he saw Slocum wasn't falling for such a quick lie. "And the ones what went blind, don't know how many of them. Folks only care about gettin' knee-walkin' drunk. This whiskey's so strong ain't many that can swill enough to actually die. Or go blind."

"Show us," Slocum said. "I want to see a bottle of it."

Pete looked around nervously, then heaved to his feet and ducked into his saloon. He reached behind the bar and pulled out a clear glass bottle filled with a pale yellow fluid.

"You got to see this." Pete sprinkled a few drops on the bar, reached up and took down a lamp, pulled off the chimney, and held the lighted wick just above the damp spot.

Slocum and Annabelle recoiled when a violent flare erupted. It settled down and burned with only a hint of blue flame before finally extinguishing itself.

"Potent, real potent," Pete said.

"I want a shot of it," Slocum said. He grabbed a glass and slid it to the saloon owner. He watched as Pete poured with a shaking hand. Slocum knocked it back—and it almost knocked him back. He had swilled everything in his day but never anything like this. He choked.

"Got the kick of a mule, don't it?" Pete said.

"Here," Slocum said, fumbling out two bits and a dime. He looked up when Pete took only the dime. "What are you selling this for?"

"Dime, same as any other whiskey."

"How can you do that?" Annabelle asked. "If you're paying twenty dollars a bottle, you're losing money."

"Even if Deutsch is selling it to you at half that, you're losing a lot of money selling a shot for just a dime."

Pete looked uneasy again, then gathered his courage and looked Slocum straight in the eye as he delivered the answer.

"I ain't payin' that. Only saloon owners who don't have Rory Deutsch as a silent partner pay that much."

Everything came together in a rush for Slocum. Deutsch would drive owners out of business selling his overpriced Taos Lightning—or they could take him in as majority owner and continue to sell at the usual rate. By doing this, he forced the other owners to either compete, go out of business, or take him in as partner. Whichever it was didn't matter since he ended up owning all the liquor establishments in town.

"You should go to the marshal," Annabelle said, staring

in disbelief. "I never thought such a thing could happen here."

"Marshal Donnelly ain't no good. He's scared of Deutsch. You ought to be, too, if you had any sense." Pete screwed up his courage and said, "Your brother didn't have a lick of sense, and look what it got him buckin' Rory Deutsch."

Annabelle hissed like a cat, spun, and flounced away. Slocum stared at the bottle of Taos Lightning for a moment, then left without a word to Pete. The bar owner called for them to forgive him, but Slocum was past that. If Annabelle heard his whining pleas, she might come back and rip out his eyes.

They returned to the Black Hole. Annabelle leaned against the bar, breathing hard as if she had run a mile. She looked up at Slocum.

"Want a drink?" he asked.

"Sure. I don't even care that it comes out of the profits," she said.

She drank down the shot of brandy he'd poured as if it were no more than water. He poured a second. She hesitated for only a moment, then downed that one, too. She sputtered, coughed, and finally got her breath back.

"Time to open the shop. Let those thirsty beggars in."

Slocum started to ask what she intended to do about the whiskey supply, then decided this was something they could hash out later. Five cases of whiskey remained in the storeroom. The Black Hole might close or perhaps it could survive as a beer bar. He had heard of special taverns in San Francisco doing that, but they were high-class and catered to people with more money than taste.

The night passed in a blur of clinking glasses and spilled beer. Once Annabelle barked at a cowboy who had spilled his whiskey, then apologized and bought him one on the house. This created a stir among the patrons. As friendly as she was, none of them had ever seen her buy a drink for a customer before. Somehow the night passed and the last customer staggered out after midnight, heading to the Santa Fe Drinking Emporium to continue imbibing until dawn.

"I don't know what we can do, John. I swear if I were a man, I'd strap on a gun and go call Rory Deutsch out."

"You'd have to take on the entire family. Just because you cut the head off a snake doesn't mean it'll die right away."

"Let it wiggle around until sundown, but it's dead eventually. They killed Tom."

"I never said that."

"It makes sense from everything Lucas Deutsch said and how you skirted the matter. Finding the road agents riding horses with X Bar X brands is evidence enough for me."

"Let's go to your house. It's getting chilly out."

She smiled, tossed a bar rag into a bucket, and headed for the door.

"Beat you to bed!"

"Don't start without me," he said.

She laughed and went out into the cold mountain air. He pulled the front door shut behind him, and they headed for her house, arm in arm. When she shivered, he realized she had left her shawl in the bar.

"I'll go fetch it," he said. "Go ahead and get a fire going."

"Don't be long," she said, "or I *will* start without you."

He retraced his steps to the Black Hole, then slowed and finally came to a halt a dozen yards away. Dark figures moved about in the space between the saloon and the bookstore beside it. Slocum slid his pistol from the holster and edged along between the adobe buildings. The rough texture cut at his back, but he never noticed anything but the three masked men in the alley behind the saloon working to light torches.

Slocum aimed his six-shooter and called, "Drop the match or I'll drop you!"

The sudden flare as one torch exploded into flame dazzled him. Then the air was filled with flying lead, tearing all around him.

6

Slocum fired but missed. This gave the three men the chance to rush him, using the lighted torch to keep him blinded and off balance. When a second torch ignited, he changed his aim slightly and fired at a point just under the ball of flame. A yelp of pain rewarded his shot. Then he found himself bowled over as two of the men hit high and low and slammed him into the adobe wall. He grunted as air rushed from his lungs, but he kept firing.

Then he shrieked as his clothing burst into flames. One torch had been thrust under his coat. Slocum clamped his arm down hard on the fiery end, jerked about, and started rolling. This would make a more difficult target for the three in the dark as well as extinguishing the fire.

He was covered in dirt by the time he fetched up against a post. He rebounded, brought up his six-shooter, ready to fire at . . .

Nothing.

The trio of arsonists had turned tail and run. He bent over, clutching his side, and moaned. Peeling away his scorched jacket revealed the singed skin. Blisters popped up and the skin was red enough to see even in the night. Slocum winched, sat up, and rested against the fence post that had stopped him. He danced between consciousness and passing out entirely.

When a wave of strength returned to taunt him, he got to his feet, stumbled out front of the saloon, and doused his coat and vest with water from the horse trough to put out any lingering embers, then used the icy liquid to shock himself completely awake. He sat on the edge of the trough, got to his feet, and managed to open the lock on the door. Inside, he grabbed a bottle of whiskey and poured a generous amount over the blistered skin.

He almost passed out, but when the initial pain died, he felt only coldness. He had driven away both pain and the chance of infection. Slocum took a quick drink from the bottle to steady himself, grabbed Annabelle's shawl, and wrapped it around himself as he left.

Slocum's pace quickened, and he felt right as rain by the time he reached Annabelle's house.

"The fire's got the place warmed up. And so am I," she called from the bedroom.

He went to the bedroom and saw a white shoulder poking out from under the blanket. She turned and revealed a tantalizing bit more. Then Annabelle sat up abruptly.

"What's wrong?"

"Brought your shawl," he said, pulling it off his shoulders. Slocum tried not to flinch but couldn't stop himself.

"You're hurt. And you smell like you bathed in whiskey!"

"I did," he said, sitting on the edge of the bed.

"You also smell like something's burned." In a lower voice she said, "Skin. That smell is burned flesh."

"Mine," he admitted. "But I ran off three owlhoots trying to set fire to the saloon."

"You stopped them from burning the building by letting them set fire to you?"

"Something like that."

"Men," Annabelle said in disgust. "Lie back. I've got some salve that'll fix you up better than a shot or two of whiskey sloshed all over your side."

The cold salve caused Slocum a moment of pain and then the last of the burning sensation vanished.

"Was it Deutsch and his brother?"

"Looked to be. Couldn't tell if one of them was the size of a mountain, but who else could it be?"

"Oh, I'll get even with them. You laughed when I said I'd strap on a gun and call out Rory Deutsch. I'll take them all on! I'll—"

"You'll do nothing," Slocum said. "This is my fight."

"Mine, too!"

"Mine," he insisted. "This isn't the first feud I've gotten mixed up in. It won't be the last."

"It had better not be, John Slocum. If you get yourself killed, why, I'll skin you alive!"

They chuckled at this. Slocum lay back, the woman's arms around him until he fell asleep.

A little before dawn, he came awake in the bed. Annabelle still slept peacefully beside him. Moving more easily now thanks to the curative power of her salve, he got out of bed and went into the kitchen. The fire had died down but the room remained warm. He took his time and wrote her a quick note using a page out of her ledger book, then strapped on his six-gun and left. He had a score to settle.

Slocum scanned the land around the ranch house, then worked to the barn. For such a large operation, the X Bar X had very few wranglers. He had spent half a day spying on the Deutsch house and had counted only a half-dozen hands, and they had been more intent on going from the bunkhouse to the barn and back without doing any work. The time in the barn amounted to less than ten minutes, no matter which of the cowboys went in. Slocum couldn't get his saddle soaped or his horse curried in that time. And no one rode out.

The ranch might be abandoned for all the activity he saw.

Most of the cowboys might be out farther west working a herd. Slocum decided to find out. He slipped back down the far side of the hill, mounted, and circled the ranch house, going far to the south and working his way through mountain meadows, which begged to have a herd grazing. He nodded in approval when he saw that none of the range had been fenced. Slocum preferred the open range to tightly penned herds. He knew some ranchers had success in dividing their land and allowing their herd to graze only a single section at a time. When the grass was close-cropped, the herd was moved to a different section, allowing the first to grow unimpeded again.

The cattle on an open range always grazed in the same fashion, and such close attention—and fencing with barbed wire, the devil's rope—wasn't necessary. Slocum thought some things were better left to nature.

He crossed a decent-sized stream and used it to hide his tracks by letting his Appaloosa splash about in the water. Who might trail him when no one expected him here was something of a poser, but crossing the Deutsch brothers had shown him how dangerous life could become. Better not to give any of them even a hint that a stranger prowled their pa's range.

He had ridden a couple hundred yards when a song drifted down from higher in the hills. Cocking his head to one side, he heard distinct lyrics almost drowned out by the rush of the water. Whoever sang had a lovely voice. Avoiding the chanteuse appealed to his common sense, but he didn't listen to his own advice. Something about the song drew him.

The singing grew louder. From the lay of the land, he thought a large pond formed at the top of a small waterfall.

Whoever sang splashed about in that pool. Letting his horse pick its own way up the slope, he entered a stand of aspens and approached from the side. Through the trees he saw occasional flashes of white skin. Bare skin. He dismounted and crept closer on foot, placing each step carefully to avoid making a sound. No Indian could have moved through the forest as silently as Slocum.

Using a large lodgepole pine trunk as cover, he peered around to take in the pool. It stretched a good twenty yards across, larger than he'd expected. The waterfall was natural. The way rocks had dammed the flow to create this pond wasn't.

He darted back behind the tree when the song lifted into a rousing chorus. Slocum recognized it as a bawdy song favored by dance hall girls.

The lyrics weren't as he remembered them. These were even bawdier and more likely to be sung at a dive along the Barbary Coast in San Francisco. Even then more than a few sailors might blush.

Rising from the water, naked as a jaybird, a woman tossed her glistening long blond hair back so that it fell almost to her behind. She squeezed out the water and partly turned until Slocum saw her silhouette. He caught his breath. Her breasts were small, firm, and the pink nipples taut from the cold water. Unaware anyone watched, she finished wringing out her long hair and began running her hands over her body. A bar of soap formed lather, which was quickly washed away every time she dipped down.

Her arms and chest received a thorough scrubbing, but Slocum felt himself getting harder as she worked the soap down between her legs. The intimate parts were hidden by the rippling pond, but his imagination took him there to the damp blond patch.

The bar of soap squirted from her hand and splashed into the pond. She bent over, giving Slocum a view of her behind. Fishing about, she successfully retrieved the soap and stood.

The sunlight glistened on the droplets all over her back, her hair, her breasts. She turned and faced him. Slocum froze like a rabbit stalked by a coyote.

She continued her song as she soaped her body some more. A final plunge and reemergence removed all traces of the lather. She worked a bit more on her long hair, then, still staring straight at him, she stopped singing and called, "You don't have to hide in the forest, jerking off. Come on out so you can get a better look."

Slocum saw no reason to turn and run like a guilty Peeping Tom. He walked to a large rock beside the pond and perched on it, drinking in her beauty as he settled down.

"Never thought I'd find a water nymph out in the mountains," he said.

"A nymph? My, a man who has read mythology. What drew you up to this sylvan pool? My singing? Did you think I was a Siren luring you to your doom?" She cut loose with another verse of the song until Slocum had to smile.

"That's enough to draw cowboys from miles off. But are you luring us all to our death?"

"Death? Perhaps it's pleasure I want to deliver to you." She cupped her apple-sized breasts, then tweaked the hard nipples until they turned red and visibly pulsed. "The idea you spied on me makes me very . . . what's the right word?"

"Excited?" Slocum supplied.

"That is close. I was thinking more of . . . outraged. A stranger doesn't come along, gawk at a lady's naked form, then have any gentlemanly thoughts left in his head. Admit it. Your thoughts were less than those to expect from a well-bred gent."

Slocum continued to drink in her sleek beauty. He found a mole lodged between her breasts that broke up the perfection, but he wasn't complaining. And she made no move to hide her nakedness.

"Reckon that's the problem. Seldom has anyone accused me of being polite and never a gentleman. So tell me. What's a gent to do when he comes across a beautiful woman bathing in the woods?"

"Ride on by. Don't snoop." She splashed about, slipping onto her back and languidly moving about to create a froth between her legs with every scissor kick. Her breasts poked out like twin peaks as she began a backstroke to move around the pond in ever-widening circles that brought her closer to Slocum. "Averting your eyes would be the polite thing to do, also."

"Good to remember," Slocum said. He stared at her as she stopped, got her feet under her, and crouched in the shallower water ten feet from him. "Should I offer you a towel? I don't see one."

"I stretch out on a rock and let the sun dry me. I don't like the feel of rough cloth against my skin."

"You must dress in fine duds."

"Silks, mostly."

She bobbed about in the water, exposing the tops of her teats and then sinking below the water again as she teased him. Slocum enjoyed the byplay, but it got him nowhere.

"You saw me when I brought the three horses back to the ranch house."

"Oh, yes, a week or two ago," she said. "You have sharp eyes to see me peeking around the upstairs curtains."

"They were lace. I saw you through them."

"As you see me through the water?"

"This is better," he said.

"I will turn into a prune if I stay in the water much longer."

She had shown no modesty up to this point. Slocum doubted she had suddenly developed a sense of decorum now.

"Rory Deutsch your pa?"

"He is. And Lucas and Timothy are my brothers. Older brothers," she hastily added.

"You know what they're up to in Taos?"

"I have no reason to ask about what is likely to be a sordid pursuit of loose women and too much alcohol."

"They're trying to monopolize the whiskey trade. Any saloon owner that doesn't buy their Taos Lightning ends up burned out or dead."

"Taos Lightning," she said, nodding knowingly. "I have heard Lucas speak of it. A vile concoction."

"Rumor has it if a man swills enough of it, he might go blind or even die."

"That is potent, indeed." She paddled around but kept her chin just at the surface of the water to maintain her newly modest pose.

"You might tell your brothers that they'll end up dead if they try to burn down the Black Hole Saloon again."

"Do you have a personal interest in it? Perhaps in the owner?"

"I *am* the owner," Slocum said.

"Not the young girl? The sister of the man killed on the road to Denver?"

"I'm the owner, and I don't take kindly to extortion."

"No," she said, eyeing him with her brilliant blue eyes, "I can see you are not the kind to be pushed around. You should know, however, that both Lucas and Timothy are terrible men. Killers. They would not think twice about filling you with lead."

"I figured that out."

"How do you intend to get back at them?"

"You have any ideas?"

"Oh, I have many ideas," she said. Her smile was about as wicked as any Slocum had seen. Her pink tongue slipped out just a bit and made a slow circuit around her lips as if she tasted him. "You might exact some revenge for them trying to burn down your saloon."

"You don't deny they tried?"

"Why, if you say they did, it must be so. You are an

impudent man, one willing to gaze at a poor young girl's bare body as she bathes, but a liar? I don't think so."

"I might be mistaken."

"That's not likely either. No, you are undoubtedly right they tried to burn you out. You might retaliate by burning down my pa's barn. That would send the proper message that you're not to be trifled with."

"I had something else in mind."

"Oh, killing them. You are both truthful and direct. How refreshing."

Slocum's hand flew to his six-shooter when he heard horses approaching. A second later came the call, "Marta, you up here?"

"My brothers. They are so protective of me." She stood, turned in a full circle so Slocum got a good look at every part of her naked body, then she screamed.

"Marta, we're a'comin'!"

She faced Slocum, smiled, shrugged her shapely shoulders, and mouthed, "Sorry."

Slocum slid off the rock and headed back into the aspen stand when a bullet ripped past his head. He ducked, dodged to the left, and put a few trees between him and the approaching brothers. They slung lead in his direction, but all Slocum could think of was the woman's name.

Marta. Marta Deutsch.

7

"He went that way, Lucas. Be careful now. He's got a gun!" Marta Deutsch tried to cover her nakedness and at the same time point. The way she waved her hand around in the air was more distracting than informative.

Slocum had to smile at the warning. The woman said nothing that shouldn't have been obvious. If the Deutsch brothers stopped to ask their sister what she was doing up in the pool, letting a stranger ogle her, that would slow them down a mite. Not much, but enough.

He cut back and went directly to where he had left his Appaloosa. The horse gave him an angry look. He patted the animal's neck, then vaulted into the saddle. He landed hard and jolted the burned side of his torso enough to remind him why he had come out there.

The men he had come to settle the score with rode after him. Slocum eased his horse around and resisted the urge to gallop off. That would have the two men on his trail in nothing flat. Instead, he moved as quietly through the forest as he could, looking for a spot to ambush the pair. The sparse copse provided little cover, forcing Slocum to ride farther upstream than he'd intended. If he crossed the stream, he could follow the Deutsch brothers' back trail.

"There he is! I kin git him, Lucas!"

Timothy Deutsch opened fire. Slocum fought to keep his horse from rearing. The bullets tore through the forest so far away from him that he knew the men only sought to flush him out if he had hidden. He kept riding until he came to the muddy stream bank and looked downstream. The woman was stretched out on a large rock, sunning herself dry as she had told him she would. She propped herself up on one elbow and waved.

Slocum tipped his hat, waiting to see if she alerted her brothers. This time she only sank back to the warm rock. She had made certain they never blamed her for not giving the warning. If they lost Slocum in the woods, that was their problem.

As he rode down the sloping trail, cutting back and forth to the meadow below, he wondered what might have happened if Lucas and Timothy hadn't ridden up when they did. Somehow, that idea bothered him. The woman was beautiful, alluring, and obviously not in the least bit modest. She might have paddled over to him and invited him join her in the pool.

What bothered him the most was Annabelle Harris. He felt he owed her something for not saving her brother, yet what more could he have done? He had not asked to be given the Black Hole. Signing it over to Annabelle would take little more than the stroke of a pen. Dr. Zamora could witness the exchange, as he had the one from Tom to him. But what more did Slocum feel for the woman?

He had had his share of women, but none appealed to him the way Annabelle did. She was feisty and took no guff off him or anyone else. She was certainly pretty and as good in bed as any woman he had come across in years.

It bothered him that if he had gone further with the Deutsches' sister in that pool, he would have been cheating on Annabelle. He wasn't married. But some bonds grew stronger than legal ones. Slocum thought on this as he rode across the X Bar X land, cutting close to the ranch house again.

He puzzled over Marta Deutsch's easy recommendation for taking revenge on her brothers. Burn down the barn? The idea had come quickly to her, as if she would do that without a second thought. Or had she only been baiting him? Her banter had shown she was an unusual woman. In her way she was as unique as Annabelle.

Slocum heard hooves pounding behind him. A quick look back showed a single rider coming after him as fast as his horse could gallop. Squinting, shielding his eyes, Slocum saw that Timothy Deutsch was pushing his horse to the limits of its endurance. As hard as he rode now, the horse would die under him within a mile. The man's bulk taxed any saddle horse.

Rather than trying to elude him, Slocum sat and watched. Because of his size, Deutsch ought to be astride a Morgan or a Clydesdale instead of a quarter horse. Neither of those draft horses showed the speed a quarter horse did, but neither would they flag and begin to stumble. Foolishly, Deutsch kept whipping the horse with the ends of the reins.

"I'll skin you alive! You're gonna pay!" The words carried across the meadow.

Slocum remained silent and stationary. He began counting backward from ten and found a small satisfaction in reaching two when Timothy Deutsch's horse died under him. The man flew over the horse's sagging head, and he landed flat on his back. The horse stumbled a few strides more and keeled over.

Killing Deutsch would be easy enough. All he had to do was ride over to the supine man and put a round or two into his bulging gut. Slocum rode off, whistling the same song Deutsch's sister had as she bathed. Some of her needling had infected him. Tormenting the brothers before seeking justice appealed to him.

But all the way back to Taos, he wondered how his life would have been different if he had joined Marta in the pool.

He rode into Taos just as the sun's daily death turned the land freezing cold. A wind whipped through the Sangre de Cristo Mountains and sent shivers up and down his spine. Slocum dismounted in front of the Black Hole Saloon and went inside. The heavy smoke had thinned because of the doors being open and the wind blowing through. For a moment he only stood and stared.

Annabelle called out, "You came back. What a surprise. Are you going to make yourself useful or do you think standing there isn't scaring off customers?"

He grinned. It was good seeing her again. It felt as if he had come home, and that thought was both comforting and frightening.

"Did a scout out west."

"I figured you were after the owlhoots who tried to torch the place. You should leave that to the law."

"The marshal won't go that far," Slocum said. He reached behind the bar and drew himself a beer. Annabelle looked disapproving, but he drank it anyway to cut the trail dust.

"Heard tell there's a federal deputy marshal on his way."

"Making a circuit or is he setting up an office here?"

"Nobody knows. Nobody knows for sure if it's even true, but rumors have a way of growing."

He bent closer and said to her, "I tangled with the Deutsches. They shot at me a few times but missed."

"And what did you do to them?"

Slocum started to reply, but the words tangled in his throat. The image of their sister naked in the pond discombobulated him for a moment.

"The big one, Timothy, chased me but his horse was too spindly and he was too big. He ran it into the ground. It took all my willpower not to go to where he was thrown and put a bullet in him."

"Why didn't you? I would have—for trying to burn the place down." Annabelle's face flushed. "He was one that shot Tom, wasn't he? You never said, but if you had horses from the X Bar X, who else could it have been? Him and Lucas and their pa killed my Tom. You should have filled him full of holes."

"I want them to know retribution's on the way before I do anything like that," Slocum said.

"I don't care. Putting them in a grave's all I care about. They killed my brother." She ground her teeth together, grabbed a damp rag, and started scrubbing invisible stains down the bar.

"Slocum?"

He turned to see a smallish man with a beer belly dangling over his gun belt. A five-pointed star was pinned on his coat.

"Marshal Donnelly," Slocum greeted him. "You come to do something about the men that killed Tom Harris?"

"Done tole you that it ain't none of my concern. I only worry about lawbreakin' in the pueblo, not out on the road."

"Miss Harris told me you'd say that."

"She's real purty, but she can be a pain in the ass with all her demands."

"Demands?"

"She wants me to go arrest Rory Deutsch and his boys."

"You're not going to do it," Slocum said flatly. "Why are you here?"

"To warn you off goin' after them boys yourself, Slocum. Mr. Deutsch, he's a real respected man in these parts. A rancher with a big herd."

"Do tell," Slocum said. He had seen scant evidence of cattle on the X Bar X. This time of year there ought to be a couple hundred head grazing up close to the ranch house and ten times that scattered through the mountain meadows.

"Real rich fellow."

"Who can buy whatever he wants," Slocum said.

"He—"

"He can even buy himself a town marshal, if he sees fit."

The lawman got red in the face and puffed himself up. He still stood five inches shorter than Slocum's six feet.

"Thass the kinda talk I came to warn you about. You can't go spreadin' falsehoods 'bout Mr. Deutsch."

"Or his boys?"

"There're back? They been gone a spell," the marshal said. Then he hitched up his gun belt. "Them, too."

"Do appreciate your warning, Marshal," Slocum said. "Can I get you a drink?"

"Drink? Why, that sounds real good. Whiskey."

"Set up the marshal with a shot, Annabelle. Since he's the law, he only has to pay the regular rate."

"What?" The lawman bristled. "You said—"

"If we're forced to buy Taos Lightning from the Deutsch boys, the price will be ten times what it is now. So enjoy the cheap whiskey while you can."

The marshal shoved the shot glass away, sloshing liquor onto the bar. He glared at Slocum, then stormed out.

"That's one thing I like about you, John. Your winning ways," Annabelle said. "You know how to make friends quick-like."

"You'd think with what Rory Deutsch pays him to look the other way, he wouldn't mind paying a dime for whiskey." Slocum took the shot and downed it.

"Marshal Donnelly came by his nickname honestly," Annabelle said.

"What's that?"

"Donkey Donnelly because he's such an ass." She slid the empty glass off the bar and dumped it in a bucket to be cleaned later.

Slocum moved away from the bar and spent the next couple hours glad-handing patrons and joshing with them to coax an extra sale or two from them. He found it easier to rope, throw, and brand calves all day long than to make small talk with the customers. When Annabelle finally threw out the last customer past midnight, he was ready to collapse.

He yawned widely. She tapped her foot and said, "That better not mean we're going home so you can crawl into bed and fall asleep right away."

"That's what a bed's for."

"That and other things. You lit out the other day and ruined a perfectly good ledger page with your note. You could have waited for me to wake up and told me what damn fool thing you were going to try."

"You'd have talked me out of it."

"Think so?" Annabelle arched an eyebrows as she studied him. "You're right. I can talk you into anything. So when we get home, I'm on top."

They locked up and walked to her house, Slocum leading his Appaloosa rather than riding. All the way, they bantered about small things, building a sexual tension that had him hopping by the time the front door closed.

She came into his arms. He kissed her, at first thinking of the naked woman in the pool and then coming around to thinking of nothing but Annabelle, slowly stripping off her clothing as she shivered in the cold. He pulled off his gun belt and dropped it on the kitchen table and began shedding his own clothes as he followed her into the bedroom.

She slipped naked between the covers. He was only a second behind her.

"On top," she insisted.

"Then we switch."

"As if you have the stamina," she said. "You've been in the saddle all day—for a couple days. You don't have it in you."

"That's because it's in you now."

Annabelle arched her back and braced her hands on his knees.

"This is going to be a hell of a night," she said.

"I'll do my best."

She straightened again, hips wiggling around the thickness hidden away inside her. Then Annabelle twisted around and called out, "Who's there?"

The doorway to the bedroom was filled with a dark figure. Slocum tried to sit up, but the woman's weight held him down at the hips. He threw his arms around her and heaved with all his strength so they both tumbled from the bed and crashed onto the floor.

But as he lay on top of Annabelle, he knew he'd been too late. There'd been a sharp *pop!* an instant before. Slocum reached around her. His hand came away sticky with her blood.

She had been shot in the back. Shot dead.

8

Slocum eased Annabelle over and got to his feet. He stared at her lifeless body. He knew he should feel something but shock robbed him of any emotion. He simply stared.

Only when he heard a six-gun cocking behind him did he turn. He balled his hands into rock-hard fists. After he finished beating the killer to death, he would mourn.

"Don't move a muscle. You do, you die."

The sawed-off shotgun never wavered. He looked from the steady weapon to the badge on the man's coat.

"Who're you?" Slocum asked.

"Federal Deputy Marshal Byron Locke. You're under arrest for murder."

"I didn't kill her. We were just in bed and—"

"This your smoke wagon?" The deputy held up Slocum's Colt Navy.

"It was on the kitchen table." Slocum's mind suddenly pulled free of shock from Annabelle's death. He knew how bad this looked. Whoever had killed her had used his pistol. All the murderer had to do was slide it out of the holster and fire. The six-shooter had been dropped back on the table for the lawman to find.

"Been fired. 'Less I miss my guess, you shot her."

"Why take it back into the kitchen, then return to the body?"

"No telling how a killer thinks. Just happened to be coming by when I heard the gunshot."

"You see a masked man running from the house?"

"No man, wearing a mask or not." The deputy stepped into the room and motioned Slocum away from the body. The lawman knelt and checked to be sure Annabelle was dead.

"The killer is getting away."

"You take one step and I'll make damned sure the killer *doesn't* get away. I'll cut you in half with this here scattergun." The deputy stood, pursed his lips, then said, "You get your pants on. I can't take you to jail naked."

Slocum began dressing. It looked bad for him. The frame was about perfect.

"Why were you coming by this time of night?"

"I got word that some fugitives I'm hunting were in town and one of them was over at the Black Hole Saloon."

"I own that saloon. We closed at midnight."

"Might be you're the one I've been tracking for almost a month. Where'd you come from?"

"I was up in Denver," Slocum said, pulling on his boots. He considered his chances of escape and didn't like the odds. The deputy showed himself to be too attentive.

"That was where the gang I'm tracking held up a couple banks. The trio worked their way south, stole the payroll from an iron mill in Pueblo, then disappeared until I got word of a man killed outside town."

"Tom Harris," Slocum said. "This woman was his sister."

"So you killed him, you and your two partners, then bedded his sister. You're a cold customer. If the letter of the law wasn't drilled into me so, I'd cut you down where you stand and save everyone the cost of a trial. But then, that would rob the judge of his pleasure. He wants to sentence you and the other two more 'n anything I ever did see."

"You travel with a judge?"

"The judge is a federal magistrate, so his jurisdiction is about anywhere he says it is."

Slocum got a better look at the deputy's badge. It matched what the man had claimed about being a federal deputy marshal.

"You two travel together, crushing crime?"

"That's one way of putting it. Get out of here. March. I got a cell waiting for you down the street."

Slocum let himself be herded along to the Taos jailhouse. The marshal was nowhere to be seen. The deputy had taken over law enforcement from the local lawman. From what Slocum had seen of "Donkey" Donnelly, it hadn't taken any argument to turn over the cell keys to the traveling federal deputy.

"You get to choose. Which cell?"

Four cages stood empty. Slocum went into the one closest to the marshal's desk. Donnelly might get careless and give him a chance to escape. All he had to do was wait out the alert deputy until the marshal came back on duty.

"He's out serving process," the deputy said, reading Slocum's intentions perfectly. "And I don't get careless." To emphasize the point, he shoved Slocum into the far cell, locked the door, stomped back, and made a big point of putting the key ring in the middle desk drawer. "Just in case you got ideas, forget them." Deputy Locke used a smaller key to lock the center drawer, then tucked the key into his vest pocket. "I didn't just fall off the turnip wagon."

"What did you say brings you to Taos, just in time to mistakenly think I killed Annabelle?"

Locke scowled.

"That was a pure coincidence. Some woman yelled out

that there was a murder going on, and I found you with the body." He pulled Slocum's Colt from his belt and laid it on the desk. "Been fired. What are the odds the same caliber bullet's in the woman?"

Locke held up the six-shooter, peered at it a moment, then added, "This looks to be a .36 caliber. Most folks now carry .44s or .45s. Makes a distinctive murder weapon."

Slocum settled on the cot and looked around the cell. It had seen better days, but getting out would be a chore if he had to dig through an adobe wall or tunnel through the rock-hard floor. From what he could see, those were more productive pursuits than trying to pick the lock or otherwise force his way through the bars.

"Hard to believe in coincidences," Slocum finally said. "Annabelle was in bed with me when somebody came in, took my gun off the kitchen table, shot her, and then fled just as you were coming in to investigate."

"Took me a couple minutes to get there."

"She wasn't dead but seconds."

"That'd mean somebody told me of the killing before it happened. How's that possible?"

"It's possible because I crossed a powerful rancher and his murdering offspring," Slocum said.

"Who might they be?"

Slocum told him of the Deutsch family, the old man and the two boys. When he started describing Timothy Deutsch, the deputy shoved Slocum's Colt back into his belt and left in a rush. Slocum stared at the outer door. It didn't quite shut and let in cold air. The stove hadn't been lit, and it was getting mighty cold inside the jailhouse. He pulled the thin blanket around his shoulders and explored his cell.

His first impression had been right. Getting free required someone to help him, and with Annabelle dead, there wasn't a solitary soul in Taos who would do so much as give him the time of day, much less risk life and limb to break him out.

"Tell me your side of the killing."

Slocum looked up. He had been so lost in thought he hadn't heard the door open and an older man come in. Heavyset with a neatly trimmed full beard shot with gray, the man stood with his feet apart and looked like he was ready to deliver a hellfire and brimstone sermon. He was dressed in a knee-length black duster that opened to show a plain vest and gold chain dangling across his belly, and his tone told Slocum he was used to instant obedience.

The other thing Slocum noted was the lack of a gun belt strapped around his waist. That robbed him of any chance of grabbing the man's weapon should he come close enough.

"Might as well save my breath for the trial."

"For the damned hanging, you mean. The deputy got you dead to rights."

"You a man who doesn't like hanging?" Slocum watched the expression on the weathered face and could not figure out what the answer might be.

"I seen plenty kicking out their last dance at the end of a rope."

"You've sentenced a lot to that fate," Slocum said. He finally pieced together the attitude and the tone. The man was a judge.

"My boy's right. You're no dummy. Quick on the uptake. Now convince me you don't think you're so smart you could get away with murder."

Slocum felt he was anything but sharp as a tack. He had missed the family resemblance between deputy and judge until now. A father and son team roaming the West, hunting for criminals to hang. It looked even worse for him, but he had no choice. Slocum detailed everything that had happened from the time he and Annabelle left the Black Hole.

"So you was buck naked when the deputy caught you with her?"

"How'd your son just happen in so quick? Who was the woman who told him of the murder?"

"I ask the questions." Again came the sharp edge of a

man who wielded power on a daily basis. "You were bare ass, the six-gun was in the other room, and the woman was on the floor beside the bed?"

"Annabelle was on top, her back to the door, when somebody burst in and shot her. I saw a shadow moving and jerked us over onto the floor."

"Much of a report?"

"No," Slocum said. "That was curious. I know the sound of my own six-shooter. It might have been a punk round."

"Or shot through a rag to hold down the noise. A rag with a hole shot through it was found on the kitchen floor."

"Why'd anyone want to do that? I expected the killer to keep shooting until he got me, too."

"You're all hog-tied and in a barrel of trouble now, aren't you? Think this might not be more pleasurable than gunning you down?"

Slocum remained silent. That much was obvious to a blind and deaf man.

"Might be these Deutsch brothers you told Byron about worked this out all by themselves."

"Timothy's not got the sense God gave a goose. Lucas is smarter, but he's the kind to just walk up and shoot me in the back. Such scheming doesn't match what I've seen of him."

"What about their pa? Rory Deutsch might be a sneaky cuss who'd take pleasure in killing two birds with one stone. The woman saloon owner's dead and the man protecting her is set to swing for the crime. One bullet gets two deaths and a powerful lot of enjoyment."

"Talked with Rory Deutsch once. Can't say if he's that sneaky a son of a bitch. I can say he is certainly a son of a bitch with the manners of a rabid dog."

The judge laughed and then nodded slowly as he stroked his beard.

"I don't think you shot her. A guilty man would have jumped at the chance to indict Rory Deutsch or his sons."

"I may be many things, but I'm not a liar," Slocum said.

"You a killer?" Judge Locke eyed him hard.

Slocum knew there wasn't anything to say. One look at his Colt showed how hard it had been used. Likely, more than one slug had been fired at another human being.

"Nope, not a liar," the judge decided.

"What are you going to do?"

Judge Locke pulled the desk chair away and planted it a yard beyond Slocum's reach, should he be foolish enough to make a grab for the man's throat. He settled himself, took out a silver flask, took a snort, then recorked it. Even watching, Slocum failed to see where the flask disappeared to when the judge had finished. He added another detail to his impression of the jurist. He might be quick on the draw if he slung iron on his hip.

"I don't know how long you've been in Taos, but not long is my guess. I've been out on the trail chasing down three outlaws from up in Denver. They robbed a couple banks, killed a half-dozen people, a couple who posed no threat at all to them, and then they lit out southward. Can't say but I think they robbed a train outside Colorado Springs."

"Judges don't usually go after outlaws."

"My son's empowered to do so, and I am a federal judge."

"What got you so riled?"

"Knew you were a smart one. Byron said as much, and I see it myself. Yes, sir. One of the men killed in Denver was a town deputy marshal." Judge Locke turned grim, ground his teeth, and then spat out, "My youngest."

"You think the Deutsch brothers and their pa might be the three killers?"

"They sound like the best suspects we've turned up in almost a month."

"They killed Tom Harris on the road to Denver." Slocum considered it. "I'm not sure if they were coming to Taos or going back to the X Bar X ranch."

"Hard to see they'd know anyone carried that kind of

money if they were coming south from Denver and he was just starting north."

Slocum had to agree.

"Might be they reached the X Bar X and heard Tom was going to Denver to buy booze."

Slocum frowned and fell silent. Things didn't set right. The killing of the whiskey peddler and the cornering of the whiskey sales in Taos had been going on while the trio was up north. Rather than poke a hole in his own theory, Slocum said, "They'll be hard to catch. They have all the bar owners in town cowed."

"Not you. You're not the kind to cut and run. You're a fighter." Judge Locke looked hard at Slocum. "More than that, you want revenge. I think you loved the woman they killed tonight."

"I wouldn't hesitate pulling the trigger if any of the Deutsch family got into my sights. Does that mean you're letting me out of jail?"

"Nope, it means I just found you guilty of murder and sentenced you to hang for the murder of Annabelle Harris!"

9

"You believe in saving money on paying juries, don't you?" Slocum said.

Judge Locke's eyes widened, then he laughed, slapped his thighs, and leaned forward. He kept just beyond Slocum's grasp.

"That's quite a sense of humor you've got."

"You expect me to tie my own noose?"

"I wouldn't go that far with any man, though I heard tell of some judges making the family pay for the rope. When a family in Arkansas refused, the judge pulled out a pistol and shot the condemned man. Then he held the family at gunpoint while his bailiff collected money off them for the price of the bullet."

"That's quite a standard to live up to," Slocum said.

"I'll talk to the editor on the paper in the morning, but by then you'll have escaped."

"How am I supposed to do that?"

"My son'll let you out when he's sure you can ride out of town without drawing unwanted attention."

"Being on the run ought to make me tolerable to the Deutsches, is that it?"

"You aren't going to leave this neck of the woods. I see it in your face. You want revenge, and this is your chance to do it all legal. Get the goods on them, bring them in, and I'll put them on trial in my court. Think of the bullets you'll save doing it that way."

"That let's both of us get our revenge." Slocum wasn't sure he liked the idea of a judge using the law for his own vengeance, though it wasn't the first time he had run across such a notion. It was certainly better than returning to Slocum's Stand and finding a carpetbagger judge ready to steal away his property. This way, he didn't have to kill the Deutsches. The legal system would grind them to dust.

He had no doubt they were guilty of a hill of crimes. Maybe a mountain, and probably one of them had shot Annabelle in the back while another alerted Deputy Locke to the crime.

"Might be necessary for me to shoot the bastards."

Judge Locke nodded knowingly and then said, "Won't hold that against you. In the eyes of the town, you'll be a fugitive, but Byron won't try overly hard to catch you. If you have to gun down any of them, I'll exonerate you as an officer of the court working for me."

"Can you deputize me?"

Slocum read the answer in the man's face. He was on his own when he went after the Deutsch family, and Judge Locke wasn't authorized to make him a federal deputy.

"I'll do it," Slocum finally said.

Judge Locke laughed again.

"You don't have any choice. You say no, you're convicted of the woman's death. A judge is impartial during a trial but that doesn't mean I can't influence the attorneys just a mite, just to keep them within the boundaries of the law."

Slocum had seen more than one judge browbeat a lawyer to get the verdict he wanted. It might take liquoring up the jury or ignoring protests from one lawyer or another, but a judge's power in the courtroom was supreme.

"When do you let it be known I'm a fugitive?"

"About any time that suits you. You realize how hard it will be for you to get in with them to get the evidence necessary for a conviction?"

Slocum knew. The Deutsches had tried to frame him for Annabelle's murder. There wasn't any good reason they would accept him into their gang. If anything, they'd be more inclined to catch him and turn him over to the deputy marshal. The same deal Judge Locke had outlined for Slocum appealed to them. They could get the law to remove an unwanted enemy. More than that, Rory Deutsch would see it as successfully completing his initial scheme since this was what he had wanted. Taking time to sort through all his impressions, Slocum thought the small man was the likely back shooter, though he had never seen his face. Rory Deutsch could as easily have killed Slocum when he gunned down Annabelle, but that took away the thrill of it.

Slocum guessed Deutsch harbored about the same fondness for the law that he did.

"How are you going to get cozy with them?" the judge asked.

"They own the liquor trade in Taos. Somewhere in the mountains they have a still going full out. That's a place to start."

"You understand what's at stake?" Judge Locke looked over his shoulder as his son came in. Byron Locke carried his sawed-off shotgun in the crook of his arm.

"He agree, Judge?"

"He's not a dull boy, son. Of course he did."

Slocum watched as the deputy unlocked the desk drawer and took out the keys. He spun and tossed the jangling ring to Slocum. Only a quick step forward and a grab through the bars rescued the keys. As judge and deputy watched, he opened the cell door. The plan was risky, and Slocum suspected a double-cross on the part of the lawman and his father, but Byron Locke handed over Slocum's Colt Navy without a word.

The gun belt felt good around his waist again. He balanced the six-shooter in his hand for a second, then crammed it into the holster.

"Give me an hour. I need supplies and a plausible story how I broke out."

"You overpowered Byron," the judge said. "Does it have to be more complicated than that?"

"Yeah," the deputy chimed in. "They don't know us. With the contempt they have for the law, they'll believe a drifter got the drop on me and lit out for the high country."

"Why didn't I kill you when I escaped?" Slocum held up his hand before either judge or deputy could answer. "I'll figure out a story to cover that. You tell about my escape and don't repeat yourself."

"Good idea," Judge Locke said. "Make it appear as to how we're covering up our own carelessness."

"Don't forget this is your scheme. I don't want to get gunned down when I bring in the three of them."

Slocum left quickly, hurrying through the gray dawn to fetch his horse. He rode to the Black Hole and got what supplies he needed from the storeroom but didn't ride out of town immediately. Instead, he stopped by Pete's. The owner of the Santa Fe Drinking Emporium slept in the rear. Slocum went around, eased open the door, and stepped into a small storage room filled with the scent of spilled beer and the sound of loud snoring.

He slipped around a pile of crates and sat on the cot next to Pete. The bar owner's eyelids flickered then snapped open. In the same instant he reached for a six-gun on the floor by him. Slocum made sure he couldn't reach it.

"Got a request of you," Slocum said. "I'm leaving town for a week or two. If you run the Black Hole, you can keep whatever profits you make."

"That's mighty generous of you, Slocum. What about Annabelle?" Then Pete grinned broadly, a gold tooth glinting in the sunlight struggling through a dirty window above his cot. "Her and you're goin' off together. Might this be a honeymoon? Ain't been a good hitchin' in town since the Armijo wedding four months back."

"Not possible now," Slocum said, shaking his head, but he didn't elaborate. "Here're the keys to the place. I'll expect everything to still be standing when I get back." Slocum started to go, then asked, "How'd the place get the name? Black Hole?"

"'Twarn't Tom's doin'. Him and Annabelle bought the place from a limey name of Cruikshank. Bugger claimed to have been in the British Army over in India. Imagine that. Another place where they call the locals Indians. Anyway, Crook, as we called 'im 'cuz that was what he was mainly, said he named it after some place in India where a passel of limeys died in a prison, all jammed up together more 'n a hunnerd years ago. Crook shoved his customers in shoulder to shoulder, so I suppose it was apt."

"Remember," Slocum said. "I'll be back."

Without another word, he made his way back through the maze of crates and got to his horse. The sun had risen far enough to bestir the town and get its citizens moving about for another day's commerce. As he settled into the saddle, he heard a loud cry.

He looked up and saw a man with a rifle drawing a bead on him. Slocum reacted instinctively. That saved his life. The bullet tore past and vanished into the cold morning air behind him.

"I got him. Here he is! The killer what murdered Annabelle Harris. I got him!"

The man worked furiously to chamber another round but the rifle jammed. The man cursed, looked up, worked more frantically as Slocum rode up and drew his six-shooter. Making a big production out of cocking it, Slocum pointed the muzzle at the top of the man's head.

"Don't go disturbing folks this early in the morning," Slocum said.

The man dropped to his knees and began praying. Slocum eased back the hammer, holstered his pistol, and rode away, aware that the Lockes had called out their posse a lot sooner than he would have thought.

This sent him thinking along other lines. Maybe it was the deputy or even his pa that had killed Annabelle. Byron Locke had showed up mighty fast after the fatal shot. What Slocum couldn't fathom was the reason. The father-son team had him dead to rights and locked away in the town calaboose. Why release him to go after the Deutsches, only to loose a posse on his heels right away?

Everywhere he looked, men glanced in his direction. He rode faster to get out of town, though his haste was due to misgivings about the Lockes' motives rather than any of the pueblo's citizens seeing him with a wanted poster pinned on his chest. Heels kicking harder against the Appaloosa's flanks, he reached the outskirts of Taos and headed into the higher slopes, west toward the X Bar X.

Getting in with the Deutsch gang would be easier if Judge Locke had killed Annabelle. This gave him a perfect reason to hunt for allies. Who better to recruit than the man who owned or controlled almost all the saloons in town? Even if Lucas Deutsch had been the one who'd shot Annabelle in the back, that made a plausible story. Rory Deutsch might think of ways of using Slocum before trying to double-cross him. As long as Slocum watched his back, he could poke around as a member of the gang.

He had convinced himself that was reasonable by the time he reached the Rio Grande Gorge and started over the rickety bridge to reach the western side. It became even likelier when his horse reared and tried to twist around. Slocum spotted four riders galloping hard for the bridge, and he doubted they were in a hurry to get across.

They were the leading deputies of the posse sent to drag him back to jail.

"Easy, boy, keep a steady gait." He guided the Appaloosa onto the bridge and started across. There might be room for two riders abreast to come after him, but not if he reached the far side. He could hold off an army from that position, though there'd be scant reason to try. Better to saw through the ropes supporting the bridge and force them to go miles up- or downstream to come after him.

His horse tried to rear as the bridge swayed in the strong winds blowing along the 800-foot-deep gorge. He leaned forward, using his weight on the horse's shoulders to hold it down. The Appaloosa calmed—but the posse recklessly charged onto the bridge.

From the way it sagged, Slocum doubted the bridge could hold the combined weight of the posse and him. He brought his mount to a trot in spite of the uncertain footing. The instant he reached the solid rock anchors on the west side, he kicked free of his horse and pulled out his Winchester. Cocking it and making a show of bringing it to his shoulder had the desired effect.

The lead deputy slowed and stopped midway across the bridge. It promised to be a turkey shoot if he kept after Slocum. The men behind him had to come to a stop. This caused the bridge to sway, straining the ropes from both the weight and the amplitude of the swing.

"Go on back to Taos," Slocum called. "If you don't, you'll be picking fish out of your teeth down below."

"You wouldn't shoot," the man said foolishly.

Slocum snugged the stock to his shoulder. If he fired, four men and their horses died. His bullet wouldn't be responsible. The huge fall wasn't anything a man—or horse—could survive.

"All right, wait, don't shoot. We give up." The deputy argued with the three crowded close behind. Getting a horse to walk backward was a challenge at the best of times. Doing it on a bridge that might give way at any instant added to the danger.

Slocum waited until the four were safely on the far side. He considered cutting through the ropes and sending the now empty bridge plunging into the river. He had a better idea.

Spare rope had been coiled beside the anchors sunk into the stone. He pulled some of it over and piled it at his feet, then pulled out the tin holding his lucifers.

"I'm setting fire to the ropes. You come across again, and you won't get halfway." He struck the match and set fire to the coil of rope. It burned brightly, thick black smoke curling upward to be caught in the gorge updraft. The fire would keep the posse at bay, but without applying a match to the actual ropes holding the bridge, it would remain in place.

By the time the posse figured out their passage was safe, he could put quite a few miles between him and them.

He rode away with the posse screaming at him for destroying the bridge. Replacing the rope required someone climbing down into the gorge with a length of rope at least as deep as the canyon, then scaling this side. Once the new rope was in place, other cables could be pulled across until the bridge was repaired.

Slocum wanted only to hold the lawmen back, not destroy a bridge that had taken weeks to install.

He cursed when he started up a long slope going deeper into the mountains. The posse had caught on to his trick and one had ridden across to stamp out the fire. As much as Slocum admired such courage, he cursed it, too. He had eight men after him now, others from town joining the posse.

The mountains twisted about and rose to dizzying heights. Slocum kept to paths that let him make the best time through canyons, though he constantly looked for a path leading to a rim. If he reached the upper wall of any of these canyons, he could lose the posse. Nothing showed that wouldn't expose him to rifle fire if the posse got close enough.

Using every trick he knew to throw off pursuit, Slocum found himself riding into a broad mountain pasture that would be his death if the posse spotted him before he reached the far side. Rather than risk the gallop across the broad grassy expanse, he backtracked.

Immediately he saw he had made a poor decision trying to find another rocky canyon that would conceal his trail. The lead riders pushed their horses to the breaking point. From the lather sloughing off the flanks, the flaring nostrils, and whites around the eyes, these horses approached exhaustion.

He realized that was part of their strategy. A few men ran him down, slowed him, let the rest of the posse on less spent horses come up and arrest him. Or string him up, depending on how pissed they were at the pursuit. While Byron Locke might be part of the band so aggressively chasing him down, he dared not count on that as his salvation. More than once he had seen a bloodthirsty posse take the law into their own hands.

Posses turned to lynch mobs mighty easy.

Too late to make an escape attempt across the meadow, Slocum angled back away from the canyon mouth hunting in the fringe of trees in the foothills for any place to hide. The pines and junipers provided some cover, but the land was stripped clean, telling him cattle grazed in the woods. This might be X Bar X land or belong to someone else. It was all Spanish land grant territory, ensuring someone laid claim to it thanks to some distant Spanish king's generosity.

He wove in and out through the trees, keeping his Appaloosa to the patches littered with pine needles. They crushed but did not show hoofprints the way leaves did. A careful tracker had no trouble following him, but he counted on the posse being townspeople bent on collecting a quick reward, not experienced trailsmen.

His horse struggled up a steep slope. The trees grew

closer together here, providing cover but making it more difficult for him to ride faster. He suddenly burst out on the crest of a low ridge.

He cursed his bad luck. A steep, rocky slope in front of him went to a river. Going either way along the ridge gained him nothing.

And behind he heard the eager shouts of a posse closing in on its prey.

10

Shooting it out meant death. Slocum had no qualms about putting a few holes in the men so doggedly pursuing him, but he saw no way to avoid being killed if he fought. He slid off the saddle and stood at the top of the steep slope. It came close to being a cliff, falling some thirty feet away to the river below. He took a last look through the woods and saw flashes of color, from the men's bandannas and glints of sunlight off their weapons.

He swatted the Appaloosa on the rump and sent the already spooked horse galloping away down the ridge. Slocum wished there had been a ghost of a chance of escaping that way. As it was, he needed the horse as a diversion. If he had stayed astride it, he would have been caught within minutes.

A deep breath, then he stepped off the rim and fell. He clamped his jaw tightly to keep from calling out or biting his own tongue when he hit. The impact almost knocked him out. The rocks slashed and cut at his back, forcing him to partially sit up. But this proved worse. The rocky slope tore at his jeans. And then he plunged into the river. The sudden cold stole away his breath.

He sucked in a lungful of water and sputtered, gasped, and floundered about as the swift current carried him from the spot where he had fallen in. He tried to blink and clear his eyes. Only blackness swirled about. His strength faded and the current felt more powerful around him. Slocum knew he was drowning. When he smashed hard into a rock, he gasped and took in even more water.

For a moment all he could do was wish for death. Then the pain hit him, forcing him to flop about like a fish out of water. His thrashing was weak. It took almost falling off a water-smoothed rock back into the water to make him realize he had been washed out of the river and was safe. He gagged and vomited up water.

He tried to push away from the rock but a strong hand held him flat. Slocum tried to draw his Colt, but the leather thong on the hammer prevented it. Coordinating his efforts became his only goal, and he failed.

"Lay still. You need to get more water out of your lungs."

He cried out as the hand shoved down hard on his back, crushing into his shoulder blades. More water gushed from his nose and mouth, but this time he felt better. Rather than fighting, he remained draped over the rock, waiting for something more to happen.

"You can get up. You're strong enough. I know it."

The hands moved over his back, tracing out the bones in his spine, kneading his muscles, moving him off the rock. He scrambled to get his feet beneath him and flopped forward onto the grassy riverbank. Only when he felt strong enough did he roll over and look up at his savior. The sun blinded him, but he squinted and turned away, looking out of the corner of his eye.

"Damn," he said.

"You could be more appreciative," Marta Deutsch said. She put her balled hands on her flaring hips and glared at him. "You have no sense of payback."

"What do you mean?"

"When you came on me bathing in the pool, I was buck naked. Here you are, sloshing around in the river completely dressed. Really."

Slocum squeezed out as much water as he could from his coat and then shucked it off to work on his vest. The woman watched him like a hawk eyeing a rabbit.

"Keep going."

"You're enjoying this too much," Slocum said, getting to his feet. He took off his vest and wrung out the water. Even so, his soaked shirt and pants weighed a ton, but the warm sun worked to dry the clothing.

"Why not?" Marta said, coming closer. She ran the palm of her hand over his chest. Streams of water ran down to his belly. With a movement quicker than a snake, she leaned over, licked up the water, then turned her face up to his. Her bright blue eyes danced. "You can't stay here." She backed away after stating what, to Slocum, was obvious.

Slocum wondered how much she knew, and if he ought to spin his yarn. She could pass it along to her father and brothers. That might make it sound a bit more *verdad*.

"What do you know?"

"Well, Mr. Slocum," she said, "I know your name. From the condition of your jeans and your coat, you slid down the cliff back at Suicide Hill. The only reason you would do that is if you were thrown. Now, unless I miss my guess and I don't think I am in this case, you are too good a horseman for that."

"So?"

"So you went down willingly. How many men in the posse almost cornered you?"

"Six, eight. I couldn't tell exactly."

"The trees. That's quite a stand of mixed conifers—those are pine trees."

"I know all about pinecones."

"I am sure you do. And piñon, along with spruce, fir, and other needled trees."

Slocum got a chance to study her more objectively now. She almost burst out of her crisp white blouse, and the jeans she wore looked as if she had been born in them. The pants were tucked into the tops of ornately tooled boots. Depending on where he rode, this style meant one of two things. Cowboys going into town on Saturday night to whoop and holler wanted to show off their fancy boots. This hardly fit Marta. The other explanation was a rich rancher asserting his authority over his hands. Wearing the pants legs so they showed off the expensive boots rather than protecting the tops showed she wasn't out on the range where they could get scratched and cut up on thornbushes or rocks.

She stood close to five-foot-five and had her long blond hair tucked up under a broad-brimmed hat. At her slender waist she wore a S&W Model 3, up high and difficult to draw fast. He doubted she needed to slap leather, but wondered how accurate a shot she was.

"Very," she said, as if reading his thoughts. "I prefer the .38 because it doesn't have the recoil of heavier models like the Peacemaker. Your Colt has been rechambered for cartridges. I believe that is a .36 caliber?"

"Did you see the posse or were you guessing they were after me?"

Marta laughed and said, "You have a delightfully one-track mind, Mr. Slocum. May I call you John? Yes, I saw them, though I did not witness your descent at Suicide Hill. That was all conjecture."

"Is there someplace to hide until the posse leaves?"

"Why, yes, the X Bar X is filled with such places. I'm sorry but I cannot direct you to them."

"I'm on foot. Anywhere I go has to be close, or they'll catch me wandering around."

"No, I don't think so. Come along. Oh, don't be so shy, John."

She took his hand after he pulled away from her. He let her lead him away from the river, up over rocks carried from higher in the mountains to a rocky ravine. During spring runoff it ran full, but this late in the year it was dry.

"You caught my horse?"

"And I brought it with me. I deduced you were in the river. I know the entire ranch, at least along the rivers since I bathe often, and knew you had to wash past this point."

Slocum went to the horse and patted its neck. He saw that the rifle was still in the sheath but the saddlebags had been removed, then replaced. The leather cords had been retied, but not as he had done before leaving Taos.

"Thanks," he said. He dropped his coat and vest across the cantle, then stepped up.

Marta smiled up at him, pleased as punch with herself.

"You owe me, John Slocum. Perhaps you owe me twice over since peeking at me back at the pond pleased you so."

"I got the feeling you enjoyed being watched then," he said. She grinned.

"I'm sure you got a feeling, but that wasn't it." Her smile melted away as she said, "You'd better go now. The posse will have reached the far end of the ridge and, not finding you, be working its way back in this direction."

Slocum took in the lay of the land. The ridge ran southwest. That had to be where the posse hunted for him, coming this way looking for his tracks.

"If I follow this arroyo east, how long before the banks drop down low enough for me to ride my horse out?"

"If you start now, you'll find out soon enough. Good day, John."

She clambered up a hillside. He watched as her jeans tightened even more, her slender legs pumping to keep her moving up the slope. It took only a couple minutes for her to stand atop the ridge. She waved to him.

Something about the way she did so reminded him of what she had done back at the pool. She had shrugged, smiled, and silently apologized as she screamed for her brothers to rescue her.

He barely rode a dozen yards when he heard Marta calling to the posse. He looked back over his shoulder to see if she sent them in his direction. This time she decoyed his pursuers away.

That was likely the difference between explaining to her brothers why she allowed a stranger to ogle her naked and a posse coming on her clothed. More than this, she could have let him drown in the river if she had meant him any harm. Slocum rode faster and found a break in the sandy bank a hundred yards farther. Scrambling up the crumbling wall, he came out on a broad, grassy stretch with a hiding place promised on the far side.

He galloped across the expanse and entered another wooded area. The hilly region provided plenty of cover. Unless the posse got lucky and found his hoofprints in the meadow, he had reached safety.

Or had he?

He inhaled deeply. His lungs still burned from the recent water in them, but he coughed for a different reason. The pungent odor caught in his throat and choked him.

Slocum had smelled this before. A slow smile crossed his lips. The Deutsches' still wasn't far off.

His horse shied from the heavy odor, but Slocum kept riding. When he came within a hundred yards of the still, he saw curls of white smoke twisting skyward. The source of Deutsches' Taos Lightning was close at hand. He dismounted but did not advance to scout the still. Instead, he worked his way back through the woods to watch his back trail for close to a half hour. He didn't want the posse surprising him at the still. Making moonshine wasn't illegal, but the deputies would partake of the whiskey, get shit-faced, and be more likely to hang him just for the hell of it.

He doubted Rory Deutsch would deny them the Taos Lightning or their pleasure stringing him up. If anything, Deutsch would take real pleasure in furnishing the rope and even in tying the noose.

Nose twitching, Slocum began the long, slow circuit of the hill where the still churned out the potent liquor. He found a trail leading off to the south. He had gotten turned around a mite when the posse chased him, but he thought the dirt path led to the X Bar X ranch house a couple miles away.

He heard a man singing off-key, missing words and generally turning himself into a beacon in the quiet forest. Slocum flopped on his belly and watched for fifteen minutes as the man chopped wood, stoked the fire under the boiler, and fed in the garbage being turned into whiskey. Old potato peels, rotting vegetables, corn husks, anything that might yield alcohol if heated enough and then the liquid distilled went into the vat. A coil of copper spiraled around, cooled by the air so the drops coming from the open end could turn from gas to liquid.

The man was shorter than Slocum by a head and scrawny as a scarecrow. He took frequent nips from a pocket flask, and once Slocum saw him refill it from the slowly dripping tube. How he kept working after drinking so much was a testament to his practice at downing such potent whiskey. Slocum had seen men like this before. Without booze, they shook like a leaf. Get a couple shots under their belt and they looked like the soberest preacher going before his flock on Sunday morning. It took a powerful amount more to get them roaring drunk.

This distiller was only starting the day and moved with the sureness of a teetotaler.

As Slocum watched, he thought on what to do. The way to hit back at Deutsch was to cripple his business. If he couldn't supply his Taos Lightning to the saloons in town, the bar owners would find their spines and hunt for other sources. Deutsch could go only so far burning out the owners and killing people. Running the businesses himself wasn't his intent. He wanted to control it, keep the owners dancing to his tune, and rake in the money.

It was simple and going his way if the still produced the hooch he forced those in Taos to sell.

Slocum crept closer. The workman continued chopping wood for the fire, but now he only split a few pieces before knocking back some of his handmade whiskey. The way he wobbled told Slocum he was crossing the line of apparent sobriety and venturing into completely liquored up. Before the sun set, he would be crawling on his belly.

But Slocum didn't want to wait that long. It was hardly past noon, and sundown, even surrounded by the tall mountain peaks, was hours off. He slid his colt from the holster, then silently cursed. The six-shooter had been soaked in the river. He should have stripped it down, dried and oiled the mechanism, and loaded it with new cartridges. The pistol might fail him when he needed it most because of his own thoughtlessness.

The distiller stopped, wiped his face with a rag, then paused, the silver flask halfway to his lips. He continued the motion, getting the flask to his lips, but Slocum knew what that hesitation meant. He had been found out.

Surging to his feet, he cocked the Colt and declared, "You'll be dead before you hit the ground if you don't get them hands up!"

The order confused the man. He stared at the flask, not sure what to do with it. Finally realizing he might get a slug through his head if he didn't obey, he stuck the cork in and then lifted his hands, the flask clutched in his left hand.

"You're makin' one helluva mistake, mister," he said. A slight slur to his words was all that betrayed his heavy drinking. "You're trespassin' on private land."

"How many gallons a week do you produce?" Slocum asked, coming closer. He looked around to see if the man had a rifle leaning against the small shed holding the still or any other firearm.

"'Nuff to keep me happy," the man said. He dropped the flask. The bright silver flash stole Slocum's attention.

And he almost died because of the misdirection. The man bent and flung his ax in one smooth movement. The ax spun about, flashing head-handle-head. Then it struck Slocum and knocked him back a step. He fired instinctively, but the dull *pop!* confirmed what he had feared. The dunking in the river had ruined the rounds in the cylinder.

But the one bit of luck came in the awkward throw. If the ax head had struck him, he would have been seriously cut. The handle whacked him in the ribs hard enough to get his attention and leave a bruise but not so hard that he added a serious injury to his already battered body.

He fired again. This round proved a complete dud. It was as if the hammer fell on an empty chamber. Then strong arms circled him and forced him back another step. The man was short and scrawny but strong from the hard work of splitting wood for the still fire.

Slocum drew up his pistol and crammed the muzzle into the man's belly as his arms tightened. Once more Slocum fired. The man grunted, although the report hadn't been any more reassuring than the two previous ones.

Bowled over, Slocum twisted as he fell and landed hard on his side. The man's right arm lay trapped underneath. Slocum used his elbow to deliver a hard blow to the man's head. This stunned him enough to release his hold. Slocum curled up, got his knee between them, and kicked as hard as he could.

The grip broke and the man rolled down the hill. Slocum struggled to his feet, the six-shooter still in his hand to face the distiller. The man clutched his gut, then pulled his hand away wet with blood.

"You done shot me. Don't feel good. Everything's leakin' out from my innards." He dropped to his knees, then bent over.

Slocum called out, "Hands up. Get 'em where I can see 'em."

The man remained doubled over, folded around his belly.

Wary of a trick, Slocum came at the man from the side, ready to use his six-gun as a club. Not a muscle moved. Slocum kicked out and pushed the man over onto the ground. His eyes were open but they saw nothing.

From the small amount of blood that had oozed out, Slocum wondered how the man could be dead. He kicked the man a couple more times to get a response. Nothing. Only then did he examine the wound. His pistol had been pointed up, not into the man's gut. The slug had little power but it was enough to puncture the skin and go directly into the man's heart.

Slocum held up his Colt and marveled at the killing power, even when it misfired. He slid it back into the cross-draw holster and went up the hill to the still. A gallon jug overflowed under the dripping tube. Slocum ran his finger around the edge and tasted it.

Even this small amount burned like hellfire. He touched his lip and knew the reason. He had split his lip in the brief fight. More of the Taos Lightning seared away an infection. Then he drank enough to pool in his stomach and create a raging forest fire. This was potent stuff.

He picked up the dropped flask, wiped off the mouth, and took another swig. This made him feel as if he could whip his weight in wildcats. He filled the flask, then tucked it into his coat pocket.

Destroying the still required no expertise on his part. He sloshed around a couple gallons of the whiskey, dripped a trail a dozen feet downhill, and then took out his tin of lucifers.

The tin was watertight as well as airtight to keep the volatile matches from igniting unexpectedly. A single flick of his thumb brought forth a bright blue flame. He dropped the match into the whiskey trail and stepped back. It burned clear and hot, working its way up to the still.

Slocum turned and ran for all he was worth and even then almost got caught in the powerful explosion. Bits of metal and garbage and fiery droplets rained down on him, making him stagger.

He looked back at the destruction. The fire built with insane fury and sent flames twenty feet into the sky. He found his horse and rode the trail toward the X Bar X ranch house.

If this didn't get Rory Deutsch's attention, nothing would.

11

Before he rode into the jaws of the monster that was Rory Deutsch and his sons, Slocum cleaned and oiled his six-shooter. It took a bit of rummaging around to find a box of cartridges in his saddlebags because everything in the bags had been pushed around. If he had wondered about Marta's curiosity, this answered it. She had searched his saddlebags thoroughly.

Colt reloaded and ready, Slocum followed the trail around and eventually sighted the X Bar X ranch house. What he intended was crazy, but sneaking around the ranch got him nowhere. If anything, it might land him back in the Taos jail when the posse blundered across him.

Slocum halted a few yards from the two-story house. He couldn't help himself. He looked up at the second-story window where Marta had spied on him before. The curtains moved sluggishly from the breeze blowing through the open window. Of the woman he saw nothing. What he felt about that remained a mystery until something more pressing commanded his attention.

Rory Deutsch came around the side of the house, head

down and hurrying along. He looked up, startled, when Slocum called to him.

"They blew it up. Your distiller's dead and nothing's left."

"What are you talking about?" Deutsch looked around as if he had been trapped. "You? You have some nerve to come back here!"

"The posse was looking for me, but your distiller took a shot at them. They killed him and blew up the still."

Deutsch stepped away from the side of the house and stared past Slocum, about where the still had been. The expression on his face was about the most satisfying thing Slocum had seen in a while. The rancher turned red in the face and bellowed incoherently.

"You have another still to produce that Taos Lightning of yours?" Slocum asked.

"Martin is dead? They killed him?"

"Reckon he's dead. Had a bullet in his gut, then the still blew up and burned him to a cinder."

"How do you know? You do it? Why are you telling me this?"

"The posse's on my trail. They think I killed Annabelle Harris, but I didn't. I got locked up for it, but the deputy marshal killed her."

Again Slocum was rewarded by the man's expression.

"The deputy killed her? Why?"

"So he and his pa could lock me up in jail. They framed me."

"His pa?"

"Judge Locke, from up in Denver. His son's a federal deputy marshal name of Byron Locke."

For the third time Slocum hit the target. Rory Deutsch's mouth opened and closed but no words came out. If ever he had seen a man stunned by news, this was it.

"You think the deputy killed Annabelle Harris?"

"It makes sense. I need a place to hide out. Might be, I can help you in exchange."

"How? You're nothing but—" Deutsch shut up when he found himself staring down the barrel of Slocum's six-shooter.

He had drawn, cocked, and aimed so fast that he doubted Deutsch saw anything but a blur.

"I'm a damned good shot, too. Want me to show you?"

"Put that away. If my boys see you with a gun on me, they'll kill you out of hand."

Slocum waited until Deutsch got a little antsy, then obeyed. He risked his neck to get evidence against the Deutsch family so Judge Locke could put them away in a federal prison, not cut him down, as appealing as that was.

"There's no need for the posse to come for me. Distilling whiskey's not a crime." Deutsch recovered his bravado and shoved his chin out, almost begging Slocum to take a swing.

Slocum wished he could. He rode a little closer and looked down on the rancher.

"Will you hide me away until the posse gives up?"

"The still's gone?"

"And the man tending it is dead." Slocum noticed that the loss of the still and the whiskey it produced mattered more than Martin's death.

"I need to get a still working again. You know anything about moonshining?"

"I'm from Georgia," Slocum said. "Seen more than my share of 'shine. Neighbors ran their own still and I helped." Slocum nodded slowly, as if considering the matter carefully. "I can set up and run a still for you. If the price is right."

Deutsch snorted and waved his hands about, as if shooing away flies.

"If I let you hide from the posse, that's pay enough."

"And all the whiskey I want."

"A gallon a week. Not a drop more. I won't have anyone drinking up my profits."

Slocum took out Martin's flask, sampled the Taos

Lightning, again recoiled from the potent liquor's kick, corked the flask, and tossed it to Deutsch.

"If he had any family, that's all that's left. I took it off his body."

"Get on up to the barn. You can stay there for a day or two. No Taos posse is lingering in these hills longer than that. They're a soft bunch."

"Offer them some whiskey, and they'll be happy to ride home," Slocum said.

Deutsch sputtered and said something Slocum couldn't hear as he rode to the barn. Slocum felt the hair on his neck rising. If either of Deutsch's sons saw him, he was a dead man. He dismounted and unsaddled his horse before leading it into the barn. Rather than tend the Appaloosa immediately, Slocum prowled about. He needed evidence, and money bags from Denver banks would go a ways toward proving the Deutsches guilty of the robbery where Locke had lost his other son.

When he didn't unearth anything, he took a quick look at the countryside around the barn. The meadow to one side sheltered a few cattle, idly grazing in the warm afternoon sun. A corral on the far side stood empty. Not far opposite it the bunkhouse and a mess hall were also deserted. From the front door to the ranch house proved equally forsaken. Deutsch had disappeared into thin air.

Slocum considered his chances of finding anything that incriminated the Deutsches and decided instead to sit and think hard on the matter. He was in the heart of the enemy's stronghold. What did Locke expect him to find? The answer that made the most sense caused Slocum to clench his fists. Judge Locke cared nothing about Annabelle's murder and everything about bringing in the Deutsch family. The only crime likely to be found out was a murder.

Slocum's murder.

Judge Locke had framed Slocum and wanted Rory Deutsch to kill him. The crimes in Denver had to go unsolved, as far as evidence that would convince a jury. Slocum hadn't heard the judge present any solid facts as to how he knew the Deutsches were even responsible. Slocum had evidence they had waylaid and killed Tom Harris, but Judge Locke didn't care about that.

If Slocum hadn't brought the three horses with the X Bar X brand back to their owner, would this have mattered? Locke wouldn't buy the lie that the horses had been stolen from a pasture any more than Slocum had. The best way to get the Deutsches on a gallows was to catch them after they murdered him.

Slocum looked out across the pasture, wondering where Byron Locke hid out. The deputy had to be close, separate from the posse, waiting to arrest Deutsch.

It galled Slocum to admit that Judge Locke had been right about his personal outrage at Annabelle's murder. If he didn't bring the killer to justice, no one would. Judge Locke wanted Deutsch. Marshal Donnelly would turn in his badge rather than go against any of the Deutsch brothers.

And Rory Deutsch would keep his iron grip on the Taos liquor supply.

Not for the first time he considered gunning down Rory Deutsch and his boys, then hightailing it. Judge Locke would have the posse after him in a flash, although his ends had been realized. Slocum saw in the man the burning need for personal revenge. If his son's killers died, good. But that would never be good enough because it robbed him of slamming down the gavel and sentencing them to hang by the neck until they were dead, dead, dead.

He went into the barn, found a piece of beef jerky in his saddlebags, and gnawed on it. Some oatmeal would go well with it, or even some of the salt pork fixed with a mess of beans, but Slocum intended to stay ready to ride out if Deutsch or his boys came after him. He knew that the rancher hadn't bought the story of how the still had been destroyed. It might take a while longer for him or his sons to poke about the ruins, but Slocum must have left some clue as to the facts. When they pieced it all together, or just because they wanted him removed as they had killed both Tom and Annabelle, he would be shooting it out.

So why stay?

Deputy Locke was out there somewhere. Riding away now would alert the lawman that he had gotten cold feet. Either the posse would be on his trail before dawn or Locke would just shoot him down, claiming he had caught Annabelle's killer. More than this, Slocum had to mete out some six-gun justice for Annabelle's death.

The sun dipped low. Slocum tended his horse, feeding and watering the Appaloosa, before looking for a place to sleep. He started to climb a ladder into the loft when he heard the steady stride of someone coming to the barn. Dropping his gear, he rested his hand on his six-shooter as Rory came in.

"You here, Slocum?"

"What did you decide?"

"I got to talk to my boys. They're both out finding stragglers and won't be back until tomorrow noon. You stay here until then. I'm inclined to take you up on your offer, but I need to let them know."

"I can double the still's output," Slocum said.

"Yeah, I'll mention that," Deutsch said. "You come on down to the house for breakfast." Rory Deutsch left without another word.

Slocum knew that he wasn't likely to make it to breakfast. If Deutsch said his sons would be back by noon, that meant sometime during the night. Why Deutsch wanted them to back him up or even do the dirty work for him was something of a puzzle. If Rory Deutsch had no trouble robbing banks and trains and killing a lawman, why worry about an interloper whom he suspected of destroying his still and killing the distiller?

The only way Slocum could find out was to play the hand

he had been dealt. He might only hold a pair of deuces, but he was still in the game.

With blanket and rifle, he climbed the ladder into the loft. Hay bales near the door drew him. A pulley and rope on an arm would give him a way out, if he had to leave in a hurry. Slocum prowled about, then spread his blanket on a pile of straw off in a corner. Rifle laid where he could grab it fast, he stretched out and stared at the rafters. A barn owl hooted and stared at him with wide eyes, then swooped down and out the open loft door.

Slocum listened to other sounds. Small critters stirring in the dark, distant lowing from cattle. So few cattle, he reflected, his thoughts beginning to drift as he fell asleep.

He came awake instantly when he heard creaking rungs on the ladder leading to the loft. The sound was slow, methodical. Finger curled around his rifle trigger, Slocum sighted in on the dark square in the loft floor. An indistinct head showed.

"You don't have to shoot me."

A hand reached up and pulled away a scarf, freeing a cascade of blond hair that turned liquid silver in the faint light as it spilled forth.

"Your pa tell you I was up here?"

"Papa plays it close to the vest. I figured it out all by myself."

Marta climbed the last few rungs and twisted about, sitting on the edge of the opening.

"Are you going to help me up like a gentleman?" She held out her hand. When he didn't budge, she said, "So? It's going to be like that, is it?"

She hiked up her feet, stood, and came to him. Her foot slid on dry straw and sent her stumbling. Slocum had no choice but to toss aside the rifle and catch her as she fell on top of him.

"So it's going to be like that, is it?" he said, laughing.

Before Marta could answer, he pulled her closer and

kissed her. She tried to force herself away, but he held her down. Her initial struggles died, and she began to return the kiss until they both gasped with ardor. Slocum wasn't sure if her tongue invaded his mouth first or a slight parting of her lips allowed him to intrude in hers. It didn't matter. Their tongues began darting back and forth, playing hide and seek, stroking, touching, tips rubbing, lips crushed together.

Slocum broke off, panting heavily.

He let Marta reposition herself, straddling his waist. She was bathed in the moonlight coming through the open loft door. He reached out and laid his hands on her breasts. Beneath her blouse he felt her heart hammering. Pressing down, he caught the hard points of her breasts. The nipples hardened even more as he tweaked them.

She closed her eyes and threw her head back, letting her hair dangle behind her. Then she jerked her head to one side and brought the hair about. With it clutched in one hand, she drew it teasingly across his face. She bent forward and worked that silvered whip down to his throat and began swishing it faster until he wanted to laugh.

"That tickles," he said.

"Does this?" She reached behind and worked to pop open the buttons on his fly.

With a quick move, she reversed her position. Still split over his waist, she bent down and used her hair to torment his already stiff organ. Every light brush across the tip, the sensitive underside, his balls, made him a tad harder. Then she bent almost double and took just the end of his manhood between her lips, using the tongue that had toyed with his only minutes earlier. Dragging her hair all around as she applied her mouth more seductively caused Slocum to arch his back.

She used her free hand to swat his thigh.

"Not yet. When you're ready and not an instant before."

Slocum closed his eyes and swallowed hard to keep control. She knew all the spots to touch to arouse him fast. But he could play that game, too. He reached out and ran his hands under her blouse, moving up her sides. His fingers traced out each rib as he went. When her blouse pressed into the crooks of his elbows, he jerked hard. Buttons popped off her blouse and rattled about.

She gasped as he reached around and caught her breasts. He mashed them flat and began rotating his palms to stimulate them. His only clue that he'd succeeded was that she stopped sucking on him because she was moaning so passionately. Her hands pressed down atop his to hold them over her breasts.

But Slocum had the advantage on her now. She had thought to keep him on a short leash, but he had turned the tables. His hands moved from her tits and down to her heaving belly. He slid his fingers into the waistband of her skirt to repeat the move. The two buttons holding her skirt in place shot like bullets as he jerked hard.

It took a bit of maneuvering to skin her out of her skirt, but he did. She hadn't worn any undies. Before he allowed her back down, he skinned her out of her destroyed blouse. Naked, she shone like a fine marble statue in the moonlight, but no cold stone met his hands as he stroked over her back, her ass, her thighs. This was warm flesh, trembling flesh under his control.

As she settled back, still facing away from him, his finger pressed into her thatched mound and finally curled about to prod into her moist interior. She shook uncontrollably now. He saw her back muscles flex and flow as he began moving her to a new rhythm of his finger slipping deeper into her core before wetly coming back out.

"Oh, John, I'm all trembly inside. Don't . . . don't do it like this. Not yet. I, aiieee!"

Her body tensed, and she threw back her head as orgasm crashed through her. Her long blond locks brushed his face again, tormented his lips with the memory of her kiss, touched his neck.

He rammed his finger even farther into her hot center, whirled it about, and then pressed into her nether lips when he retreated. Her body shook as if she had a high fever. He ran his left hand up and down her back, tracing out each and every bone in her spine. It was as if his fingers set off new explosions of delight within her. Every time he pressed down, she groaned and jerked about. He kept up the steady movement of his finger in and out of the tightness between her thighs, but her climax had passed.

She was more in control now as she reached down and stroked from the base to the tip of his hardness. It was his turn to surrender. She used her fingernails along his upper legs, every scratch fire and every touch pure pleasure.

When she caught him, lifted her hips slightly, and slipped back down, he felt himself entering paradise. Her tight warmth surrounded him totally. Tensing and relaxing her strong inner muscles gave him a new type of massage he would never forget. The aching in his length as she began twisting her hips from side to side turned to outright pain.

"Can't take more of this. Move, damn you, move!"

He circled her waist with his hands and lifted. She resisted at first, then allowed him to set the pace. He started fast and worked to a pitch that had them both crying out once more. She clutched down all around him with her inner muscles an instant before he erupted. Her fingers stroked his balls even as her depths milked him for every drop held there.

He arched his back as she slammed her hips down. They ground together, separated, and tried to continue, but both were too spent. Marta leaned forward, her rounded behind taut for him to stroke across. She gripped his ankles, then worked her way back to a sitting position.

"You fell out."

"You wore me out," he said.

"For the moment?" Marta lifted one slender leg and spun about, facing him now. "How long?"

"You're mighty persuasive," he said. "Why don't we find out?"

She slithered like a snake down between his legs so her head disappeared between his thighs. But he knew exactly where she was—where her mouth was. She kissed and licked and sucked until he was ready again.

This time the lovemaking lasted far longer. The urgency had passed and each one tried to show tricks and touches, kisses and caresses the other didn't know. Slocum doubted either of them learned anything new, and it hardly mattered by the time they lay entwined, arms and legs wrapped in a pretzel.

Slocum dozed but came awake when he felt the woman disengaging from the amorous Gordian knot. He muttered as if he still slept, watching her the best he could as she gathered her ruined clothing. Marta crept naked to the ladder, looked back at him, blew a kiss, then disappeared into the barn below. He strained to hear her bare feet on the floor. She moved too much like a blond ghost.

He stretched, then rolled onto his side to get some real sleep. But it eluded him. Brushing away the straw on the loft floor gave him a spot to press his ear. Distant sounds alerted him that someone was moving about beneath him.

Slocum hastily dressed and fumbled around for his rifle in the dark. He found it just as a head poked up through the trapdoor.

A bullet ripped past him and tore a splinter in the barn wall. Slocum wasted no time triggering a round from his rifle. The foot-long orange muzzle flash dazzled him. He hoped it blinded his attacker as much, but from the new fusillade tearing toward him, he doubted it.

Slocum crouched, spun about, and then launched himself out into space through the loft door.

12

Slocum strained to grab the rope. It fluttered just beyond his fingers. He started to fall. His rifle tumbled away, but he concentrated completely on the rope hanging from the loft pulley. As he fell, he twisted. Behind in the loft came angry cries as the Deutsch brothers scrambled through the trap-door in pursuit.

He fell and then at the last possible instant caught the rope and jerked around hard. His hands slipped, leaving rope burns on his palms, but the plunge had halted. Slocum swung out, then came back toward the barn as bullets ripped the air around him. This time he let go of the rope that had saved him from a nasty fall and dropped a few feet to the ground. His hand flashed to his six-shooter.

He drew and fired almost parallel with the barn wall. His slug missed Lucas Deutsch as he leaned out the loft door, but it didn't have to hit him to halt the deadly rain falling on his head. Deutsch ducked back inside, giving Slocum the chance to scoop up his rifle.

He held it close to his body, then rolled on his shoulders and came to his feet just inside the barn in time to see feet groping for the ladder from the loft. He fired. His first round took off a boot heel and brought forth a long, loud string of curses. The second round he put through the flooring just to the left of the trapdoor brought a groan of pain. He knew the injury wasn't serious. It didn't have to be.

A few precious seconds had been bought with that round. He saddled his horse, fired a couple times through the loft flooring, then swung up and galloped from the barn, bent low and angling away to prevent Lucas from getting a good shot from the outer loft door.

Lead sang through the air but came no closer to him than a few feet. Then he rode out of range. Cutting across the pasture, he headed for the woods a quarter mile off. Before he reached the safety of the copse, hoofbeats behind him warned of pursuit.

He rubbed his crotch, remembering the night with Marta. Had she only kept him there until Rory Deutsch found his boys and sent them to kill him, or did she enjoy the lovemaking? He had gotten a great deal of pleasure from the coupling. She was energetic and inventive. But the fact remained that she had kept him occupied so her brothers could fill him with lead after she left him in the barn.

Slocum slowed and finally came to a halt to rest his horse. The Appaloosa's sides heaved from the effort of getting to safety. Slocum swung about in the saddle and looked at his back trail, waiting for the brothers to come into view. It wasn't sporting, but he was all out of fair play. If they showed their ugly faces, they'd get them blown off.

His rifle pulled to his shoulder, Slocum gave up after a few minutes. There had been no mistaking the hoofbeats pursuing him. That meant they tried to circle and cut him off. He considered thwarting them by riding back to the ranch house and capturing their pa. Rory Deutsch had sent his boys out to do his dirty work. It seemed only fair if he got pulled into this deadly hide and seek.

A horse pushing through thick undergrowth to his left

alerted Slocum to the approaching brothers. He had been right. One came from his right flank and the other from his left. They thought to get him in a cross fire. If he played his cards right, he could slip away and let them shoot each other.

Going back across the meadow would expose him to both men's fire. But riding straight through the woods had been left open as an escape route for a reason. They knew the ranch better than he ever could. They wanted to herd him forward.

Slocum decided to fall into their trap, whatever it might be.

He rode slowly until he came to the edge of the woods, where he could see how the land dropped off as suddenly as it did at the Rio Grande Gorge. The cliff was hardly a hundred feet above a river, but he had no chance to slide down it as he had the similar incline Marta had called Suicide Hill. This was too steep, too far, and the last time he had gotten lucky with the woman pulling his ass from the river.

He would never survive the fall from this cliff. With two angry, armed killers behind him, fighting his way to freedom looked impossible. Slocum kicked his feet from his stirrups, then carefully stood on the saddle. The horse shifted uneasily under him as he reached up and caught a limb.

His fingers barely curled around the pine sap sticky branch, forcing him to jump. As he did, his horse neighed loudly and trotted forward. Slocum dangled from the limb for a moment, then kicked hard, got a leg over the branch, and pulled himself up to lie flat. The green wood began yielding under his weight. The tip dipped down and the slender limb shook, about to tear free from the trunk.

Slocum kept his weight as spread out along the branch as he could. It still trembled as if caught in a high wind when Lucas Deutsch rode beneath him.

"There's his horse," Lucas shouted. "Don't see where he got off to. You see him, Tim?"

"Naw. Got a shot at the horse."

"Don't kill his horse, dammit. That's a fine piece of horseflesh. It'll bring a pretty penny in town."

"Where'd he go, Luke?"

"Don't know. He musta gone over the cliff edge, but why he'd try to kill himself like that's a poser."

Lucas Deutsch rode a few yards farther. If he moved any more, Slocum would lose his chance. With all his strength, Slocum kicked away from the pine tree and crashed down. He misjudged his fall and his intended target.

His hands raked Deutsch's back rather than grabbing his neck. All that saved Slocum was the sticky sap. His hands pulled the man's coat away from his body enough to get a firm grip. As Slocum fell to the ground behind Deutsch, he yanked hard on the trapped coat. The man exploded off his horse and sailed through the air.

Slocum thrust his hands into dirt to get rid of the sap, then went for a struggling Lucas Deutsch. The outlaw had landed on his left shoulder and thrashed weakly, grabbing for it as he moaned.

"Move and you're a dead man," Slocum said, pointing his Colt at the fallen man.

"You busted my shoulder. You busted my damn shoulder! Tim! *Tim!*"

Slocum kicked and landed the toe of his boot on Deutsch's chest. This knocked him off balance—and saved his life. Timothy Deutsch opened fire. The man's shots went high and wide but would have winged Slocum if he'd remained standing. He sat, kicked Lucas Deutsch again just out of spite, then took careful aim on the hulking man a dozen yards away.

The sap on his fingers betrayed him. Slocum cocked the Colt, but his thumb stuck. He triggered a round and missed by a country mile. Timothy Deutsch returned fire, then wheeled about and galloped off, running out of range before Slocum could cock the pistol a second time.

"You busted my shoulder," moaned Lucas Deutsch, still weakly wiggling in the dirt.

Slocum grabbed him by the shirtfront and lifted. From the way his face turned white, the pain overwhelmed him. Slocum paid no attention as he shoved Deutsch along to where his horse nervously pawed the ground.

It took only a few seconds to reach the animal, but this gave Slocum all the time he needed to decide what to do. Chasing Timothy Deutsch would be more dangerous than the pursuit merited. He had one of the Deutsch brothers. Using him as bait to draw in Rory and Timothy would work.

"Get up there," Slocum said, shoving Lucas forward.

The man passed out. Slocum knelt and lifted an eyelid. This wasn't a charade. He had conked out. Finger probing Deutsch's shoulder told the story. He had dislocated the joint when Slocum pulled him from horseback. The distinctive feel convinced Slocum he had to do something. Deutsch wasn't going to die, but riding wouldn't be possible either, unless he was draped over the saddle and taken into town that way. Doing so slowed the trip and gave his brother and father a chance to rescue him.

Slocum sat with Deutsch on his back. He gripped his wrist and put one foot in his armpit and the other on the side of his face. Slow, steady pressure straightened the arm and pulled the arm out enough so it snapped back into place. Deutsch never regained consciousness but the loud *pop!* along with the way his entire body went limp told the story. Using the arm anytime soon would be painful, but he could ride.

Slocum slapped him a couple times until his eyelids fluttered.

"Get in the saddle. We're riding back to Taos."

"Ride?" Deutsch sat up and rubbed his shoulder. "Hurts like hell. Can't ride."

"Then I'll shoot you right here," Slocum said, brandishing his six-shooter. This got Deutsch to his feet.

Slocum retrieved his Appaloosa and rode back to where Deutsch struggled to mount. The man finally oozed up and into the saddle.

"You're a dead man, Slocum. If I don't kill you, Tim will. And if he don't—"

"Shut up. If you don't, I'll yank that arm back out of joint."

Lucas Deutsch grumbled but not loud enough for Slocum to make out the words. He got his bearings and started back for Taos, prisoner in tow.

"You imbecile!" Judge Locke raged. "There's nothing to hold him on. I have to let him go! You didn't find one whit of evidence he or his brother or pa killed my son!"

"There wasn't any evidence to be found," Slocum said.

"They murdered him!" Judge Locke paced across the small jailhouse office. Marshal Donnelly edged to the door and fled into the night. Locke never noticed.

"I wasn't able to do a complete search, but I couldn't find anything to even show they'd robbed the bank. No money bag with a Denver bank logo, no mail pouches from a train robbery, nothing."

Slocum stewed in his own juices. Expecting the Deutsches to keep any evidence of their crimes was ridiculous. They'd stuff money into their own saddlebags and ride, not bothering with the bulkier canvas or burlap sacks. He thought Judge Locke raged now because his plan had fallen apart.

He had expected the Deutsches to kill Slocum and leave evidence enough to bring them to trial. Bringing one of the gang back didn't fit into his cockamamie scheme.

"The posse's still out in the mountains hunting for you. I offered a dollar a day with a fifty-dollar reward if they brought you back."

"You posted more for me than for him." Slocum jerked his thumb over his shoulder in Lucas Deutsch's direction.

The man sat in the farthest cell, his arm in a sling. He mumbled constantly about what he'd do when he got free. Slocum had heard about every torture there was. Deutsch invented some new ones to inflict on Slocum.

Slocum had to smile. What more would the man do if he found Slocum had spent some intimate time with his sister not once but twice? It would infuriate him even more if Marta told him how much she liked it.

Of course, she might lie. The first time Slocum had seen her bathing naked in the pool, she had sicced both brothers on him to protect herself. Denying the night spent with him in the barn wouldn't be any more difficult a lie for her than how she had wantonly displayed her bare body in the pond.

Slocum's thoughts wandered when he realized how he had been attracted to Marta then, and how he would have turned her down if she had made the same offer she had in the barn or out by the river. Slocum hadn't been married to Annabelle, but he might as well have been from the way his behavior had changed. And now she was dead.

Slocum looked hard at Judge Locke, who dropped heavily into the marshal's chair and glared. Framing him for killing Annabelle fit better with the judge's plans than it did with anything the Deutsches might do. He didn't see any of the three men as being that subtle. Timothy wasn't too bright, Lucas whined a lot, and their pa hardly seemed a mastermind plotting intricate crimes.

Any of them would have walked in on Slocum and Annabelle and plugged them both.

"You don't have to charge him. Let the gossip do your work for you. Spread the word that he killed Annabelle and is going to trial for it."

"I'd have to get word to the posse that you're not wanted anymore," Locke said.

"Spread the word in town. Rory will hear and come for his son. Trying to break a prisoner out of jail isn't the same as bank robbery or murder, but it's more than you've got on him now."

Calculation flashed in Judge Locke's brain. He might as well have spoken aloud because Slocum knew what he was thinking from his changing expression. If Rory and Tim Deutsch came for Lucas, he could gun them all down and stay within the letter of the law. Why that mattered to him puzzled Slocum. He had seen judges aplenty willing to step across the boundaries of the law to satisfy themselves. As hard as it was to believe, Judge Locke might consider the law sacrosanct and hunt for ways to remain on the right side.

"They come for him, we're waiting. But they'll expect us to guard him real close."

"That won't stop them. This is a matter of honor." Slocum hesitated, then added, "Just as it is bringing them to justice for your son's murder."

He could have offered a dozen other arguments, but this one struck the bull's-eye with Locke.

"The posse would be good to hide all around the jail, but they're still out hunting for you."

"Too many men will scare them off. The marshal, you, me, your son. That's all we need. It'll be four of us against two of them, and we know they'll be coming."

"They'll know we're ready for the attempt to spring him, too." Judge Locke scowled in Lucas Deutsch's direction.

"Get the word out now, while men are still in the saloons. There's no surer way of telling them what you intend."

"They won't believe a word of it!" Lucas Deutsch shifted about on the cot. "They're too smart by half."

"Good thing I put him in a cell without a window so he can't shout that outside," Locke said.

Slocum opened the door and dragged Marshal Donnelly back inside. The marshal had been spying, his ear to the door. Slocum's hand stuck to the lawman's coat, in spite of rubbing as much of the pine sap off as possible.

"The judge's got something for you to tell around town." Slocum stared at his hands again. "I need to get some kerosene to soak off the sap."

"Sap," shouted Lucas Deutsch. "That's what you are, Slocum. The rest of you, too. I'll be out of here before dawn! Mark my words."

Judge Locke spoke rapidly to the marshal, who grew increasingly frightened.

"We gotta hold the prisoner 'gainst the Deutsch clan? That's suicide!" Marshal Donnelly turned pale and swiped his hand across a sweaty forehead.

"We'll be ready. You go tell everyone Slocum's cleared of Annabelle Harris's death and that I'm holding Lucas for it." The judge pursed his lips. "Go on. It'll be fine. You come right on back. Sober."

Donnelly looked like a prairie dog as he left, his head bobbing up to look around, then dipping down, only to pop back up a few paces farther down the street.

"He's a weak link, Slocum."

"He'll do his duty," Slocum said, more for Deutsch's benefit than to mirror the truth. Given the chance, "Donkey" Donnelly would bray and kick and run like hell from any trouble. "I'll let Deputy Locke know what we're planning."

"Do it after you get that pine ooze off your hands. There'll be plenty of time to set the trap."

Slocum left, the night air invigorating him. The notion of all the Deutsches behind bars appealed to him, especially if Judge Locke charged them with Annabelle's murder, even if they didn't do it. What rankled was the notion the deputy had pulled the trigger—or the judge himself. Slocum knew he had to be sure before riding away from Taos. Annabelle's killer wasn't going to get away scot-free, whoever it was.

As he went in search of some kerosene, he had to wonder if Locke would press that charge to the fullest. Slocum couldn't shake the feeling the judge had been responsible for killing Annabelle and framing him to use as a cat's-paw in his determination to bring the Deutsch gang to justice.

He found a kerosene lantern in the livery stable and sloshed the liquid on his hands. The pine sap peeled away easily when he rubbed his hands on a rag. As he worked, he realized he hadn't figured out Judge Locke yet. Did the man step outside the law to bring his son's killers to justice or not? It made sense to Slocum that he or Deputy Locke had shot Annabelle, but wouldn't it be quicker if they just rode up to the Deutsch ranch and opened fire? With a posse backing them up, they could cut down the entire family.

That was a possibility if Judge Locke ignored the letter of the law. If he adhered closely to it, someone else had killed Annabelle. And that had to be one of the Deutsch boys.

Or Rory Deutsch himself.

A last swipe got the kerosene off his hands. Slocum wiped down his six-gun to be sure the hammer and trigger were free of the sticky sap. After checking the load, he walked back to the jailhouse. The stars were a brilliant blanket overhead, giving him enough light to walk easily.

He turned the corner and started for the jail when he saw three horses outside that hadn't been there before. Slocum broke into a run when a single gunshot rang out. He threw down on the masked pair leaving the jail, with Lucas Deutsch trailing them.

He fired at the biggest of them. He recognized Timothy Deutsch's shout of defiance. Slocum fired until his six-shooter came up empty and still he ran. The three rode off in a cloud of dust.

Slocum kicked open the jail door. Marshal Donnelly lay facedown in a pool of his own blood. From the look of it, the single shot had drilled smack through his forehead. In the rear, a single cell door stood open, the key ring swaying gently from the key in the lock.

They had come for Lucas Deutsch much sooner than he had expected.

13

"He's dead," Judge Locke shouted. He pointed at the marshal's body on the floor as if the lawman were in contempt of court. "I should never have let you talk me into such a harebrained scheme."

Slocum had never known Marshal Donnelly, but Annabelle's opinion of him had been lower than a snake's belly. That didn't mean he wanted to see the lawman dead, especially when the trap had been sprung too soon. That much of the judge's scorn he had to bear. Dealing with the Deutsch family had shown him how dangerous they were. He should have known.

"They got to town mighty fast," Slocum said. "I hadn't been back a couple hours and Rory Deutsch was already here to spring his boy."

"I heard tell that Deutsch was in town earlier today. He might have figured out what had to be done when the other one showed up."

Slocum nodded.

"There's no doubt that Timothy Deutsch was one of them springing Lucas," Slocum said. The man's bulk was as distinctive as if he had worn a Union flag wrapped around his shoulders. "They both wore masks, but the other one had to be Rory Deutsch. I recognized his horse, a paint with a patch on its rump."

"I'll get my son and we'll go after them. I can find the posse. We'll burn the son of a bitch out if we have to." Locke stepped over the marshal's body on his way outside.

"Something doesn't fit," Slocum said. He tried to put into words the uneasy feeling that he was missing something important.

"Rory and Timothy Deutsch broke Lucas out of jail. Marshal Donnelly's dead. What's wrong with you?"

Slocum started to speak, but Judge Locke stormed away. Pulling up the marshal's desk chair, Slocum sat and stared at the body, as if the corpse would come alive and tell him what he missed. It was as straightforward as Judge Locke said. Timothy Deutsch was quickly identified because of his size. Rory Deutsch's horse was as characteristic. Lucas was gone. One had killed the marshal, and it mattered naught which had pulled the trigger. In the eyes of the law, they were all guilty.

That was enough for Judge Locke. Why wasn't it enough for Slocum?

He heaved to his feet, skirted the drying blood on the floor, and looked around before leaving, homing in on the Santa Fe Drinking Emporium across the plaza. The gaiety had died down and Pete had only four customers. Two snored at a table, a deck of cards and stacks of poker chips ignored. The other two stood at the far end of the bar, arguing in a friendly way. Slocum saw nothing to hint at sudden death here.

"You outta the clink? Fancy that." Pete bent down behind the bar.

"Leave the scattergun where it is. Judge Locke decided it was one of the Deutsches that killed Annabelle."

"Now why'd they go and do a damn fool thing like that?"

"Tom wanted to buy liquor from a dealer in Denver, and

so did she. Rory Deutsch's monopoly on the town's whiskey supply was threatened."

"One tiny crack in the wall can spread," Pete said, nodding. He stood. "You want a drink?"

"Not the Taos Lightning that Deutsch sells you," Slocum said. "That's too strong for me. A beer."

As Pete drew the beer, he said, "Rory don't have no trouble drinkin' his own swill. I never seen a man who could put it away. He was in here all afternoon. He was half my business."

Slocum said nothing. This was an instance of the owner drinking up the profits since Deutsch had cut himself in as a silent partner in the cantina. Pete would have gone out of business without the cheap whiskey.

"I do declare, he put away damned near a full bottle of that 'shine."

"When did he leave?"

"Couple hours back."

"He must hold his liquor well," Slocum said. Rory Deutsch hadn't shown the least bit of drunkenness as he mounted and rode away from the jail after rescuing Lucas.

"Don't know 'bout that," Pete said. "The door wasn't close to bein' wide enough when he left. A while back, a week or two 'fore Tom was killed, Rory spent the day in here. It took three of his wranglers to get him on his horse."

"They get him back to the X Bar X?" Slocum frowned as he sipped the tepid beer. Again that mental itch bothered him, and he didn't know where to scratch to ease his mind.

"Suppose so. Ain't my part to see customers get home, even if one of 'em's the owner. The silent partner, at least."

Slocum heard the bitterness in the saloon keeper's voice. Pete had little in the world but his pride in owning the Santa Fe.

"Hey, Slocum, I got a few bucks for you. From the nights I ran yer place 'til the whiskey run out. Didn't see no reason to peddle only beer, and I didn't know how Rory would take it if I used some of the Santa Fe's 'shine over at yer place."

"Hang on to it," Slocum said. He had forgotten about the Black Hole. "I don't know when I'll get back to it. I need to—"

Slocum looked up into the mirror behind the bar to see Judge Locke run in. The man's face was flushed, and he gasped for breath.

"There you are, Slocum. He's gone."

"Lucas Deutsch?"

"No, you idiot, my son. Byron!"

Slocum glanced at Pete, who stared wide-eyed. He began wiping down a beer mug without actually seeing it.

"I ain't seen him since earlier, Judge. He was in here 'bout the time Rory Deutsch was," Pete said.

"He took out after Deutsch. They have him. You got to get him back, Slocum. This is all your fault. You made a complete mess of it."

Slocum's anger rose, but he held his tongue. Arguing with the judge got him nowhere. If he pointed out that the Deutsches had no reason to take the deputy marshal prisoner and would have killed him outright, Locke would have slapped him back in jail. The law ceased to mean anything compared with revenge.

A whole indigestible lump of vengeance rested in the pit of Slocum's belly. For the good deed of bringing Tom Harris to town to die, he had wandered into a real shit storm that never stopped. The one good result had been Annabelle, and she'd caught a bullet in the back because of him.

"Did Rory Deutsch say anything about hightailing it?" Slocum asked Pete.

"Nope. All he went on about was fixin' his still. The old one got blowed up, from the hints he dropped. The man is obsessed with makin' 'shine, but then that's 'bout all he does that amounts to a hill of beans. Heard tell the X Bar X is hurtin' from his poor management. Even heard the last of his wranglers have drifted on, but I can't testify to that for certain sure."

"They took Byron when they broke Lucas out of jail," Locke said, cutting off Pete's gossip. "You have to rescue him."

"How do you know he isn't on their trail? What makes you think they took him hostage?"

"Hostage for what? They sprung Lucas." Judge Locke's florid face turned whiter than bleached muslin as the obvious hit him like a freight train. "They'd kill him, wouldn't they?"

"So he's on their trail," Slocum said. "That ought to make finding him easier. The Deutsches will leave tracks and so will he."

He drained his beer and left the judge with Pete and the other customers. The night air he drew into his lungs cleared his head. Byron Locke might have gone after the gang by his lonesome. Chances were better that he had caught a few bullets and lay dead along the trail. Slocum fetched his horse, got supplies for the chase, and rode from town a little before dawn stroked the sky with pink and gray fingers. A storm formed over the Sangre de Cristo peaks in front of him, making it even more important to get on the trail before rain obliterated every trace.

He spied on the ranch house for over an hour and never saw movement anywhere. The entire Deutsch family had abandoned it. Slocum hoped to find one of them and sneak along on his back trail to find the deputy. He had failed to find any trail at all of the Deutsches or Locke from Taos so he decided that his best option was to watch and wait. Catching a glimpse of Marta Deutsch again wouldn't have been so bad either.

Slocum wondered if he could get her to help him. She knew how dangerous her brothers were. The way she disappeared just before they showed up with blood in their eye proved that, but the lovely woman hadn't shown any hint that she would turn them over to the law. She helped Slocum get away from them, but she always covered her own sweet ass first.

Venturing closer, he made a quick search of the house. Downstairs gave him nothing, but he lingered in Marta's bedroom. He hadn't expected to find a room quite this plain. Such a pretty woman surrounded herself with pretty things, knickknacks, porcelain, and lace. He hesitated rummaging through the wardrobe, yet he found himself driven to do so. The clothing hanging inside was simple, with more sturdy clothing suitable for riding than he'd expected. He even found a duster with what looked like a bullet hole in the canvas.

Slocum snorted in disgust at himself. The room looked more like an austere hotel room than a woman's—and he was pawing through her belongings like some sneak thief. He closed the wardrobe door, looked at the neatly made bed, and wondered how it would be with Marta in bed rather than in the hay or on the cold, rocky ground. Someday he would have to find out.

After finding nothing to help him in the other rooms upstairs, he went to the bunkhouse. The X Bar X had once employed as many as two dozen wranglers from the number of beds he found. Now the cobwebs and dust told a different story. Deutsch had either fired them, or they'd drifted away. He chalked up Pete's gossip as being the gospel truth.

That meant the X Bar X was no longer a working ranch but instead had become an outlaw hideout. Rory Deutsch made more money selling his Taos Lightning in town than he could in a good season of cattle raising. Slocum had tallied up the numbers, and Deutsch rivaled any of the land grant owners in wealth because of his moonshining and extortion.

The crates given to the cowboys to stash their gear were all empty. He sat on one and stared around him. This ranch had been a big one in its day. Selling Taos Lightning had proven more lucrative than the backbreaking work of raising cattle.

His hand flashed to his six-gun when he heard a rider approaching. Slocum went to the bunkhouse window, rubbed away a spot on the dirty pane, and saw Rory Deutsch heading for the barn. The rancher hurried, telling Slocum he had to act now.

Before he could race outside to get the drop on Deutsch, the man had mounted and ridden off to the south, the barn blocking his departure. Slocum ran to get a better look. It was Rory Deutsch, all right, but he rode a different horse other than his paint.

Unable to capture him here, Slocum knew the next best thing would be to track him to wherever he and his boys had made camp. Finding Byron Locke alive wasn't too likely, but Slocum could lasso the trio and drag them back to Taos for Locke to pass judgment on them.

How best to go after Deutsch caused Slocum a few seconds of consternation. Riding hard then sticking a pistol under his nose to force him to tell where his sons were had advantages, but when Slocum galloped across the pasture, he discovered that Deutsch had vanished. He slowed and finally dismounted to look for tracks in the grassy meadow. The turf had been cut up by dozens of horses crossing, making it impossible to tell which set of hoofprints belonged to Deutsch.

Then Slocum's nose twitched. A familiar smell caught on the breeze and blew straight for him. Deutsch had his still running again, only in a different location. Caution told him to approach without being seen to find what he'd got himself into. Slocum's usual patience abandoned him. He rode straight into the woods, homing in on the heady smells of distilling Taos Lightning.

A curl of smoke from the center of the woods confirmed what his nose told him. Slocum slipped his pistol from its holster and braced it on his saddle horn as he made his way through the trees.

Ahead he caught sight of a horse—it wasn't Deutsch's.

He walked his Appaloosa to a point where he saw the still in a small clearing. The horse had been tethered next to a lean-to. Slocum would have bet the Black Hole Saloon that Deutsch had ridden from the barn, but he came around to believing he was wrong. Someone hired by the rancher might have gone to fetch supplies, then come straight here. But he didn't see the man anywhere.

Knowing his quarry had to be inside the small shed built for the still, Slocum rode closer and brought his six-shooter up.

A flash of motion out of the corner of his eye brought him around. Rory Deutsch disappeared into the woods. It had to be Deutsch. The rider wore the same duster Slocum had seen the rancher wearing when Lucas was busted out of jail.

Slocum considered capturing yet another distiller working for Deutsch or going after the rancher himself.

He tugged on the reins and got his Appaloosa trotting through the woods after Deutsch. The man had to lead Slocum to his sons' camp—and maybe even Byron Locke.

14

Slocum lost Rory Deutsch's trail within minutes. How the rancher managed to fade into nothingness as he had angered Slocum. He counted himself better than most trailsmen and the equal of the rest. It shouldn't have been possible for Deutsch to up and disappear as he had done.

Riding into a meadow, Slocum looked around. The still lay a couple miles behind. From here, he barely made out the curls of smoke rising from the fires feeding the distillation process, and the pungent odors were swallowed by the fitful wind. Craning his neck, he strained to hear any hoofbeats. The rising wind muffled such noise and robbed him of a powerful tracking method. The way Deutsch had ridden made it unlikely he knew Slocum was anywhere near.

So how did he get swallowed up by the forest so quickly if he didn't try to lose anyone on his trail?

Slocum wiped his face with his bandanna, then settled his agitation to concentrate. Deutsch hadn't tried to lose him because Deutsch didn't know anyone was out in the forest. Or did he ride to throw Deputy Locke off his trail? The judge could have been wrong that the Deutsch gang had taken his son prisoner. That never made a whit of sense to Slocum. Rory Deutsch would gun down the deputy and leave him where he fell. Or he might take him with him, then dump the body into the Rio Grande Gorge. No one would ever find it once the raging river carried it downstream.

Slocum put his heels to the Appaloosa's flanks and walked toward a stand of junipers that must have been Rory Deutsch's destination. Slocum realized he might have missed catching the man at the still by only minutes. He cursed his bad luck, and then he realized Lady Luck smiled on him instead.

By losing the tracks on the larger trail, he had wandered too far west and only now came along a small game trail. The trail where Deutsch had ridden had been rigged with a devious trap. A thin strand of rope stretched from one side of the trail to the other. Anyone not knowing it was there would have broken the string. As it was, Slocum had come up past the trap and saw the way the rope had been wrapped around the backside of the tree and up to a shotgun tied to the tree limb.

Blunder across the trigger, get a load of buckshot in the face.

Deutsch had something ahead to protect. Slocum advanced along the smaller trail cautiously, alert for any other traps. He had hardly ridden twenty yards into increasingly thick forest when he heard voices ahead. The argument grew heated. Slocum came to the edge of a clearing hardly a dozen feet across. In the center a cooking fire worked to heat a coffeepot dangling from an iron tripod. To the far side a crate had been opened.

Slocum saw the stack of supplies there, telling how this was a semipermanent campsite.

Timothy knelt by the fire, poking at it with a stick and trying not to look concerned at the fight between Lucas and his pa. Slocum drew his rifle and considered what he could do. Timothy Deutsch was an easy target. Lucas stood holding the reins of his pa's horse and Rory was completely hidden behind it. Slocum might shoot the man in the leg between the paint's legs, but it would be tricky since the horse would rear and Lucas might be able to return fire in the confusion.

"Aw, come on," Timothy Deutsch complained. "Will you two stop arguin' so much? You're givin' me a headache."

Lucas responded by raising his voice. Rory Deutsch's was muffled and sank to only a low murmur.

"Dammit, we can't do that. We got a federal marshal on our asses," Lucas said. "If you hadn't busted me outta jail, Judge Locke woulda swung me for sure."

Again Slocum couldn't hear Rory Deutsch's reply. The paint started pawing the ground and complaining. Slocum sat a little straighter and raised the rifle to his shoulder. From the way the campfire smoke blew, he had suddenly become upwind from the horse. His scent spooked it. If he didn't act quickly, all three outlaws would go free.

"Don't," came the low voice behind him.

Slocum swiveled, the rifle training on Byron Locke. The deputy marshal motioned Slocum to retreat.

"They're all here. This is our best chance of taking them together," Slocum protested.

"Don't have enough evidence. Not yet. I need to know where they hid the loot from the Denver job."

Slocum backed away, then followed the deputy deeper into the woods away from the Deutsch gang. He seethed. Even if he had let one of them go, he knew two of the road agents would be dead by his hand. He still worried the Lockes might have had something to do with Annabelle's death, but he knew the Deutsch family had killed her brother. That might not be good enough for a court of law, but it was for him.

"What makes you think there's any evidence left?" Slocum asked when he and Locke were far enough away that the dense forest muffled their voices. Even with the wind blowing in the direction of the camp, they were safe enough. "Even if the banknotes from the robbery were issued on a Denver bank, that's not real proof."

"I didn't want you shooting them out of hand. I need a confession." The deputy looked earnest.

Slocum remained silent. Getting any of the Deutsches to confess to murdering a lawman was nigh on impossible. The deputy had to know that. Even a confession gained by torture wasn't going to be enough for evidence in a lawful court.

"What do you have in mind? There are three of them, two of us."

"They don't know we're here—or that anybody's on their heels."

Slocum remembered the booby trap set on the forest trail. The Deutsches showed foresight enough to ensure their own safety, or at least time to escape if the need arose.

"We can always make them think there are more of us than there are," Slocum said. "Set up a rifle with a string on the trigger, fire it, and then rush in from other directions."

"I'm not giving up my rifle for a single shot." Locke clutched his rifle until Slocum wondered if he'd leave fingerprints in the stock.

"The big one's tending the cooking, Lucas and their pa were talking to one side of the clearing."

"Clearing's only a few yards across," mused Locke. "They might escape into the woods. If nothing else, they have handy places to extend a fight."

"We come at them from opposite directions," Slocum said. "When they take cover against one of us, the other gets the drop on them from behind."

Locke nodded slowly, his lips working but no sounds coming out. He finally looked up and nodded a final, assured gesture.

"Good idea. I'll circle. I want to get the drop on them myself."

Slocum doubted the deputy trusted him, but he only wanted this done with. The quicker they moved, the sooner the trio would be in custody and Slocum could get on with his life.

He waited for Locke to mount and ride off into the dense

woods. He took out his pocket watch, flipped open the case, and studied it as if he had never seen it before. This was his brother Robert's sole legacy, and every time he stared at the ornately engraved case or the roman numerals around the dial, he thought of him. Slocum blinked and got out of his reverie. This time as he stared at the hands moving as if dipped in molasses, he had the chance to settle himself.

After five minutes, he thought Locke had plenty of time to get into position. Slocum hefted his rifle, walked back to the clearing, leaving his Appaloosa out of the line of fire. A quick look made him wonder if any time at all had passed. Timothy Deutsch still poked at the fire, and Lucas and his pa still argued.

Slocum thought a single shot would cut the legs out from under Rory Deutsch. The paint crow hopped and made such accuracy chancy. As he pondered taking the shot, Timothy Deutsch looked up and let out a whoop.

"Slocum! He's found us!"

The giant of a man went for his six-shooter. Slocum shifted his aim from Rory Deutsch's knees to smack dab in the middle of his son's massive body. His finger came back, the rifle bucked, and Timothy Deutsch grunted, then sat heavily. He looked down stupidly, reached up, and brushed at his chest with the muzzle of his six-gun. Then he collapsed in the dirt.

"Hands up!" Slocum shouted to empty air.

As Deputy Locke had anticipated, the others had ducked into the woods, using the thick-boled trees as cover. Slocum worried that Rory Deutsch had gotten his horse out of the line of fire. He tried to find the man in the woods but couldn't. Foolishly sticking his head up almost got it shot off by Lucas Deutsch.

Slocum ducked back and got off a couple rounds to keep Lucas from noticing Byron had sneaked up on him. It occurred to him to shoot low. Random lead sailing over Lucas's head might endanger Locke.

"You're not going anywhere, Deutsch," Slocum shouted. "Your brother's dead."

He glanced at Timothy Deutsch and realized it took more than a single bullet to kill that hulking giant. Feeble kicks turned stronger until Timothy flopped onto his belly and started crawling for the underbrush.

Slocum edged around. Shooting a wounded man in the back wasn't his style, but for Timothy Deutsch he made an exception. If he hadn't been the one who had murdered Annabelle, he had taken part in the frame-up. Slocum braced his rifle for the killing shot, only to be startled when he heard Byron Locke cry out in pain.

"They got me, Slocum! They got me. Shot me clean through the leg. Take 'em down. Take 'em all down!"

The deputy's voice cut off suddenly. Slocum jerked around and fired at the escaping Timothy Deutsch. His shot missed. Then he dove for cover as two six-shooters opened up on him. He had Lucas's location pegged, but where was Rory?

"I can't let you back-shooting sons of bitches go," Slocum called. Insults meant nothing. He wanted Rory to reveal himself so he could get a better shot. Kill the father, maybe Lucas would get so mad he'd make a mistake.

Slocum liked the idea of Lucas Deutsch charging head-long at him to avenge his father's death.

Nothing of the sort happened. Try as he might, Slocum failed to see the slightest movement in the brush that gave away Rory Deutsch's position. A couple shots where he thought the man might be hiding failed to flush his quarry.

Slocum ducked down when Lucas began firing with more accuracy. One bullet tore away a splinter just inches in front of his nose. Slocum wiped away sap, then emptied his rifle's magazine before switching to his six-gun. He took only two shots before realizing something was wrong.

"Deutsch?"

Nothing. Slocum threw caution to the winds and rushed across the clearing, vaulting the low fire and iron tripod with the coffeepot swaying beneath it. He crashed through the undergrowth. Nothing.

The Deutsches had escaped.

Slocum circled the area like a caged animal, muttering to himself as he pieced together what had gone awry with the attack. Byron Locke had been caught by Rory Deutsch. From the evidence, the deputy had been tossed over his saddle and led off. Slocum saw tracks of two horses leading away. Working farther afield, he found a trail of blood from Timothy Deutsch's chest, but he also saw where the man had mounted and ridden away in a different direction.

Lucas had stayed as a rear guard, then hightailed it, too, leaving Slocum alone at the camp.

Slocum got his bearings, knowing he had to rescue the deputy from Rory Deutsch, hiked to his Appaloosa, and mounted. It took the better part of ten minutes to find the trail again.

And he lost Deutsch and Locke within another ten minutes. That Rory Deutsch had evaporated into thin air made Slocum angrier than ever. This time he had the deputy as his prisoner, and Slocum was left with no way of finding him.

"A swap," he said to himself. Resolve hardened as he swung his horse around and set off through the forest, wary of other shotgun traps.

He found two others along the biggest game trail. Why a deer or wolf hadn't triggered the guns was something of a mystery, but wildlife had a way of surviving. One season he had spent the winter trapping in the Tetons and had almost starved to death and hadn't bagged more than a dozen pelts. The critters had outwitted him at every turn.

Just as Rory Deutsch was doing now.

Slocum finally reached the meadow, where he spotted the curls of smoke rising from the hidden still. The only one with a connection to the Deutsches he could find was whoever tended the still. His value as a trade for Locke was questionable, but Slocum had nothing more. All his cards had been played and his chips shoved into the pot.

He found the place where he had started his futile hunt for Rory Deutsch, then worked his way to the still. Heat from the fire made him sweat, even at twenty feet away. His Colt Navy slid from the holster, and he dropped to the ground.

"Lucas, that you? I—"

Slocum fired as Rory Deutsch came around the shed holding the still just as the rancher went for his six-shooter. Slocum missed, and so did Deutsch. The difference came in Deutsch having the shack to use as cover. He slipped around the corner, then opened fire.

Exposed and out in the open, Slocum fell forward and braced his six-gun with both hands, his elbows digging into the soft dirt. He sighted carefully, forcing himself to bide his time. His most recent mistakes had all come from rushing. Calming himself, he squeezed back slowly on the trigger.

It discharged. His reward came in a loud yelp. Deutsch dropped his six-shooter and left the shelter of the shed to grab for it.

Slocum squeezed off another round. This one hit Deutsch in the shoulder. From the shriek of pure pain, Slocum knew he had busted his shoulder joint. Deutsch would be lucky to ever use his arm again.

"Stay where you are or the next shot will blow the top off your head," Slocum said.

He got his knees under him, then rose to his feet. The entire while he kept his pistol trained on Deutsch. After going to him and kicking away his six-shooter, Slocum said, "You're in sorry shape, but then the deputy's not likely to be better off."

"The deputy? Locke?" Deutsch stared at him with a mixture of confusion and loathing.

"I'm swapping him for you. If he's dead, that's the way your boys will get you back."

Slocum grabbed Deutsch by the collar and heaved him to his feet. The man was shorter than he remembered.

And he wondered how Deutsch had swapped his paint for a roan. Slocum wondered about that as he scribbled out his ransom note and stuck it on a nail for Lucas and Timothy to find.

15

Slocum kept an eye peeled for the Deutsch brothers, but mostly he rode behind Rory Deutsch and puzzled over the horse the man rode.

"How'd you get to the still so fast?" Slocum finally asked. "You kill the horse under you?"

"I don't mistreat my horses. But I swear, when my boys catch you, I'll use a horse whip on you until the skin falls off your back."

"How bad is he hurt?"

"Who are you talking about? That deputy of yours?"

"Timothy," Slocum said.

"You plug him?"

"Wasn't the deputy that shot him. Locke came up from behind. I had a good shot at your boy and took it before he got feisty."

"Shot him from ambush, more 'n likely. That's the kind of coward you are."

"No worse than putting trip wires across game trails. Triggering a shotgun blast like that kills a man without knowing he's even in trouble."

Slocum watched Deutsch's shoulders draw back as he rode a bit prouder. Something in the reaction seemed odd to Slocum. It was as if he didn't know anything about the booby traps. How he had reached the camp with his two sons might have been along a different path, but the one Slocum had seen with the shotgun was the most direct between still and camp.

He frowned as he considered that. Why hadn't his sons simply camped out at the still? There wasn't any call to go hide in the woods.

"What are you planning on, Slocum? Shooting me in the back?"

"That's not going to free Deputy Locke," Slocum answered. "You're my poker chip, and I'm trading you for the lawman."

"You're swapping a white chip for blue? That's rich." Deutsch laughed a little too loudly, putting Slocum on edge.

He studied the terrain more closely. Deutsch tried to hide some small sound with his nervous laughter. They were a couple miles from the X Bar X ranch house, where Slocum intended to trade the man for Byron Locke. Blundering into the Deutsch boys before he got there would ruin his plan. He needed a safe position to conduct the swap. If they rode straight to the house, they would arrive before him but wouldn't see the note that he had taken their pa as prisoner.

"What are you going to do if they killed him? The deputy? They don't have any love for the law, much less carpetbagger deputies."

"You better hope they haven't killed him," Slocum said, but he considered how easy squeezing the trigger and leaving Rory Deutsch dead might be. Killing in cold blood came easy for some men. Not John Slocum.

Deutsch laughed again, too loud to be natural.

Slocum saw movement off to the right, just behind a sparse stand of pine trees.

"Ride!" Slocum swatted Deutsch's horse on the rump

and sent it galloping. He bent low over the neck of his Appaloosa to present as small a target as he could. They crossed the meadow and hit a double-rutted road, kicking up dust that shielded them from sight.

Deutsch tried to veer away several times, but Slocum had worked the range too long to let a stray get away from him like that. The road curved and then the X Bar X ranch house loomed ahead. Slocum took a quick look around but saw no one moving about. Rather than the brothers reading his demand note, they had either stumbled across him as they rode or had come directly here and he crossed their path.

"To the barn," Slocum said.

As he came up behind Deutsch, he stared at the loft door swinging in the wind. The wooden arm holding the pulley looked forlorn. The rope he had used to get away from Lucas and Timothy Deutsch before still lay in a pile on the ground. The memory of what he and Marta had done in the loft convinced him that not all the Deutsches were out to kill him.

"Inside," he said. When Rory Deutsch hesitated, Slocum swung hard, connected with the man's cheek, and knocked him to the ground. Deutsch groaned and tried to sit up but failed.

"Can't move. You blew my shoulder to hell. Now my leg's all bent up."

Slocum jumped to the ground, grabbed Deutsch by the collar, and dragged him to the barn door. He checked the man and saw he had told the truth. His arm hung useless and the fall had broken the right leg. Deutsch wasn't going anywhere.

Slocum led his and Deutsch's horses into the barn, retrieved his rifle, and loaded it. The last shell slid into the magazine when Lucas Deutsch trotted into the yard in front of the house.

"You got our pa. Let him go and we don't kill the deputy."

"Send Deputy Locke out where I can see him."

"We ain't killed him, not yet. But we will."

"Your pa's got a game leg," Slocum said. He pulled the rancher out and let him flop about just outside the barn door. "Send the deputy over and we'll swap."

Lucas started to argue, then wheeled about and rode around the house where Slocum couldn't see.

"I hope they kill that damned deputy," Rory Deutsch grated out. "I hope to hell they kill *you!*"

"They try either of those and you're a dead man."

"It's worth it if I know you'll be waiting in hell for me."

Slocum put the rifle muzzle against the man's head as Lucas rode back around.

"Deputy's all trussed up like a Christmas goose. We ain't freein' him from his ropes so you can trick us."

"Get him out where I can see him."

Lucas motioned. Timothy rode half bent over, clutching his belly where Slocum had shot him. Behind trailed a horse with a man slung facedown over the saddle. Slocum recognized the lawman's clothing but couldn't tell if he was dead or alive.

He had gotten himself into a tight spot. Shooting his way out made for a risk he refused to take unless he assured himself all three of the Deutsch family died on the spot. Rory was in a sad way, and Timothy had been gut shot. Slocum had seen men survive for a week or more before infection took them. Timothy might be on that road. That left Lucas, but the way the outlaw cleverly positioned himself, any shot Slocum made had to be past Byron Locke. The short range favored a single killing shot, but the horses milled about uneasily.

"I'll get mounted. I'm leaving your pa where he is. You set the deputy's horse to running and I'll catch up to it."

Lucas tilted his head as if listening, but Timothy said nothing. His only contribution was a low groan as he clutched his belly.

"Get mounted," Lucas said. He paused, then added, "And you better ride like you mean it."

Slocum got his Appaloosa from the barn and swung into the saddle. He stared at Rory Deutsch. If looks could kill, Slocum would be dead a dozen times over.

"You need some of that Taos Lightning you're fixing up. That'll do for you real good," Slocum said.

Then he was galloping after Locke's horse. Lucas had slapped its rump and sent it running full speed. But as Slocum rode after, a shot rang out. He looked over his shoulder. Lucas had already reached his pa and knelt on the ground beside him. Timothy wobbled in the saddle.

Another shot tore past Slocum. He saw Byron Locke jerk, then spastically twitch. Bending low, he dodged back and forth in a zigzag pattern to confound the sniper. No more shots came. Slocum reached out and snared the reins and guided the horse toward a ravine. Once in the arroyo, he slowed and finally brought Locke's horse to a halt. The animal's flanks heaved and its nostrils flared. It took all his skill to even get close enough to drag the deputy from the saddle.

Locke slid to the ground. Under his weather-beaten skin, he had turned pale. He reached out with a shaking hand, grabbed Slocum's coat, and pulled him close.

"Don't let me die, you son of a bitch."

"You're too consarned mean to die from a single bullet," Slocum said, seeing only a single bloody spot on the man's back.

He rolled Locke over and tore away coat and shirt.

"You're hardly wounded at all," Slocum said. "The bullet broke skin but only went a half inch into you. Slug must have come from a punk cartridge." He took out his knife, stretched the skin tight around the hole in the deputy's back, then pressed. Locke screamed. Slocum pressed harder and then dug the knife point under the small-caliber slug. It popped out into his hand.

Slocum displayed the bloody hunk of lead for the deputy to see.

"All removed. You're more scared than hurt."

"I'll kill you for what you did!"

Slocum shoved the deputy flat on the ground and stood, towering over him. The knife dripped blood onto the lawman's chest. If it were possible, Locke turned even paler.

"You settled down?" Slocum asked. He slid the knife back into its sheath, then reached down, grabbed Locke's hand, and pulled him to his feet. The deputy almost fell, but Slocum kept him upright.

"Let's go back to Taos," Locke said between clenched teeth.

"I got the slug out of you. You hit somewhere else?"

"Town," Locke repeated.

Slocum let the deputy wrestle himself back into the saddle. Locke had put a dozen yards between them before Slocum stepped up and got his Appaloosa trotting along the sandy-bottomed ravine. The deputy's back was a bloody mess. If Slocum hadn't seen it with his own eyes, he would have thought the man had died from the wound. Either extreme range or punk powder had kept the slug from drilling too deep into his skin. That failed to explain his choler toward Slocum.

They found the road from the X Bar X that led into town. Slocum weighed the chance of going back and capturing or killing the three Deutsches. With Rory all laid up and Timothy carrying a bullet in the gut, catching Lucas would be a breeze. Seeing how Locke wobbled in the saddle now and again warned Slocum a better course was to get the lawman patched up. Once he had begun to mend, they could go after the Deutsch gang.

Slocum barely slept that night, every sound a potential warning. And when the sounds died, he came fully awake. For no good reason. The night was as barren as a whore's compassion, leaving him almost as woozy as Locke when they hit the road the next morning.

By noon, they rode up to the Taos jailhouse and dismounted.

For the first time since escaping the Deutsches, Byron Locke looked alert.

"Your pa's not inside," Slocum said, looking through the open door. The large dark stain on the floorboards marking where Marshal Donnelly had died gave mute reminder of how dangerous a game they played. "I can go look for him."

Slocum turned and stared down the barrel of his own rifle. Locke had reached over and yanked it from the saddle sheath.

"Drop your smoke wagon, Slocum. Handle that gun real slow, or I swear, you die on the spot."

"What's gotten into you?"

Locke levered a round into the chamber. Slocum had something new to worry over. The man was not only pale but his trigger finger trembled. Such a dangerous combination spelled death. He did as ordered.

"Kick the gun away." When Slocum did, Locke came over, bent low, and grabbed the Colt. "Now, I—"

Slocum moved like a striking rattler. He grabbed the deputy's wrist and wrenched it back. The sudden gasp of pain told him he wasn't hurting the man as much as prior injuries were. That didn't keep him from pressing Locke back even more, but the lawman's determination knew no bounds. He twisted about and got his finger around the Colt's trigger.

"What's going on here?"

The question caused Slocum to glance over his shoulder and see Judge Locke hurrying up.

The brief loss of focus on Slocum's part almost proved deadly. Locke drew back the Colt's hammer. The hammer fell and detonated the round in the chamber. The slug missed Slocum's face by an inch and caught the brim of his hat, knocking it back off his head. Too much to deal with all at once forced him to wrestle with Judge Locke when surprisingly strong arms circled his body, pinned his arms, and then threw him off the deputy.

Byron Locke sat up, cocked the Colt Navy, and held it in a shaky hand.

"I'll shoot, Slocum. I can't miss, not at this range."

"What the hell's going on, son?" Judge Locke stepped out of the line of fire. "Why are you holding him in your sights?"

Slocum tried to decide what his chances were against the trembling deputy, then decided he wasn't in any position to get away without catching at least one round from his own pistol. That riled him as much as the deputy's sudden change of heart.

"I brought him back after the Deutsch boys bunged him up," Slocum said. "I swapped Rory Deutsch for him and now he wants to shoot me!"

"I heard them talking, Pa," Byron Locke said, scooting to prop himself against the jailhouse wall. He steadied his hand on a bent knee, taking away any chance Slocum had to escape. "He's part of their gang."

"They've tried to kill me. I would have killed them if I had a chance. I put a round in Timothy Deutsch's belly. Why would I go and do a thing like that if I was in cahoots with them?"

"All I can think is that was a mistake on your part. You might have been aiming for me and Deutsch got in the way," Byron Locke said. "I want him in jail, Pa. If we can't get the rest of them, we'll at least have him."

Slocum knew better than to argue. Whatever Locke had overheard had either been confused or something the Deutsch brothers deliberately said so he would turn on Slocum. Either way, the result was the same.

Slocum walked into the jailhouse, the deputy and judge close behind.

16

"They were lying," Slocum said to Judge Locke. "Everything they said about me was intended to make your son think I was riding with them."

He hung on the cell bars, watching how the judge reacted. It looked bleak.

"They expected to kill Byron," Judge Locke said. "No reason for them to be so cunning. Besides, which of them thought it up? From everything you say, Rory Deutsch is the brains of the outfit."

Slocum started to answer, then pursed his lips. Something fluttered across his mind, just beyond his understanding of what it might be.

He finally said, "Lucas isn't as stupid as he acts."

"That boy shoots first and thinks on it later. That's one reason I want him swinging from the end of a rope." Judge Locke turned even more dour. "You said you plugged Timothy?"

"Got him in the belly."

"Byron claims Deutsch only pretended to be shot to make it look like you were on our side and not theirs."

"I didn't miss," Slocum said. "He's just dying slower than I expected."

"Moreover," Judge Locke went on, not hearing Slocum, "Rory was with you when they spilled their guts about you being part of the gang."

"How's that make any sense? I brought Tom Harris back after they shot him. One of the Deutsch gang shot Annabelle in the back."

"About that, might be Byron had the right idea at the time. If you killed her brother so you could be with her, then you might have killed her when she found out. That's a powerful argument for you killing both brother and sister."

"I never met either of them before I came across Tom being robbed out on the road."

"So you say. The trial will bring that out. You want me to find you a lawyer or you got one in mind already, Slocum?"

He had nothing to say to that. Locke, like his son, had passed beyond listening to reasonable arguments. The evidence piling up on Slocum's head was featherlight. A good lawyer could blow all the fluff away and lay bare the truth. Slocum settled on his cot and stared through the iron bars. That presented the biggest hurdle he had to getting free.

He needed a lawyer who believed him. Unless the Lockes had passed around the word that Slocum had been working for them while the posse scoured the mountains for him, most of the town still believed he had shot and killed Annabelle. Even if the lawyer made all the right arguments, finding proof for it bordered on the impossible. With a jury already questioning his innocence, Slocum worried that he might get his neck stretched long before any of the three Deutsches.

"I reckon we can get the trial started in a couple days," Judge Locke said. "That ought to give your lawyer time to get all the evidence he needs."

"Two days?" Slocum knew railroading when he heard it.

Again something struck him as odd about Rory Deutsch,

but Judge Locke's rush to start the trial worried him more now. It might be that Locke intended using Slocum as bait. If he believed his son—and Deputy Locke believed what he had overheard—Judge Locke might be using Slocum to lure the gang in to rescue him. If that were so, Slocum would be dancing at the end of a rope with the Deutsches laughing as they watched his execution.

"Reckon I've been wrong in my approach to the law," Locke said, picking his teeth with a wood splinter as he stared hard at Slocum. "An old man gets impatient. That's what happened to me. Getting my only living son all shot up convinces me I need to go slow, take my pursuit of justice a tad slower."

"So you'll hang me, then go after the Deutsch family one by one?"

"Can't say that's wrong. If I remove you thieving murderers one at a time, that's eventually as good as doing it all at once. For all I know, it will be more satisfying." He spat out the wood. A sneer came to his lips. "Though seeing the lot of you strung up side by side would do an old body good."

"So much for a fair trial. You've already convicted me and sent for an executioner."

"I'll tie the noose myself. Won't be the first time." Judge Locke spun about and left, slamming the jail door behind as he disappeared.

Byron Locke had been carried over to Dr. Zamora's surgery, so that had to be where the judge was going. Or maybe his departure signaled the setting of the trap. Slocum rattled the bars, hoping that was so. If Locke wanted immediate justice, letting his prisoner escape so he could be gunned down before hightailing it out of town seemed a clever trap.

The cell door rattled but did not budge. Slocum examined every inch of the cell and found no weakness he could exploit. He had been put in the back cell, the one without a window, so prying loose the bars from the thick adobe walls wasn't open to him. A thorough examination of the outer wall and the floor showed no hint of a hole being started or a tunnel dug out in the rock-hard floor. Slocum flopped back and worried that the judge didn't intend to use him to draw in the gang but fully expected to hang him.

Slocum rubbed his grimy neck. He had come close to dangling before and had vowed to avoid that fate. Unless he came up with something brilliant in the next few minutes, that promise to himself was likely going to be broken—along with his neck.

He sat up fast when the office door slammed open and a gust of cool breeze whistled through. The bright sunlight outside turned the figure in the doorway into shadow. The man stepped back, motioned, and then made way for Lucas Deutsch. Slocum couldn't mistake him for anyone else.

Behind Lucas in the doorway leaned his brother. Timothy stood partly bent over, but from the way he gripped a scattergun, he was miles away from being dead. Right now Slocum didn't know how he felt about his earlier failure to kill the giant.

"Where'd they put the damn keys?" Lucas yanked out drawers and let them crash to the floor as he hunted.

"Middle drawer. Locked," Slocum said. He watched as Lucas pried open the drawer and snatched the keys. With an expert spin, he sent the ring whirling and stopped it only when the proper key came up between his fingers.

"You do that like you have some experience," Slocum said.

"Shut up. We were told to get you out. That doesn't mean I got to like it one damn bit." He tossed Slocum's gun belt and pistol to his brother.

"Your pa wants me out?"

Lucas crammed the key in the door lock, inclined his head toward his brother, then turned the key. The cell door swung open easily. Timothy covered Slocum so he couldn't jump his brother.

"You want to stay in there?" Lucas asked.

"No matter what you have in store for me, I'm not inclined to stay one second longer," Slocum said, pushing past Lucas. Timothy had already gone back outside.

Slocum saw him knocking out the rounds in the Colt's cylinder. Timothy shoved the Colt Navy back into the holster before tossing it to Slocum. It felt natural weighing down on his left hip, though he had to reload before that weapon mattered more than a hill of beans.

"Mount up. We're getting the hell out of Taos now."

Slocum's Appaloosa pawed at the dusty ground, where it had been tied to an iron ring. A quick mount and Slocum was ready to ride. He caught sight of Rory Deutsch's paint vanishing down a winding street leading toward the plaza. Before he could start after the man, he caught sight of both Lockes. Judge Locke worriedly watched his son stumbling along under his own power. About the time he spotted them, Byron Locke saw him and went for his six-shooter.

Faster than thought, Slocum reached for his six-gun, then remembered Timothy had unloaded it.

"Back to the ranch," Lucas said.

Slocum bent low as the deputy marshal began firing. For a man in his weakened condition, Locke's aim was damned good. The judge's shouts faded, but the warning rang in Slocum's ears for a mile down the road.

The judge had told his son to stop firing and to get the posse ready to hit the trail of "the goddamned road agents" again.

Slocum saw that Timothy rode ahead of him while Lucas brought up the rear. He slowed his headlong pace a quarter mile west of Taos and then began angling away. Lucas would have none of it.

"You ride with us."

"Judge Locke's getting a posse together to come after us. Even if he can't prove you killed Tom Harris and his sister, you're guilty of breaking a prisoner out of jail."

"Never killed the bitch, though I wanted to," Lucas said

sourly. Louder, he called to Slocum, "I was told to keep you with us all the way back to the ranch."

"Why does your pa want to see me again? After I tried trading him for the deputy, I'd think he would want to see me dead."

"Don't know what he wants. I know he's pissed how you burned down his still and left him a cripple."

That struck Slocum as curious. Again the gossamer touch of memory caressed his mind. Then it all vanished as distant gunfire sounded.

"Damnation, Slocum, you was right. They got a posse after us quicker 'n I thought possible." Lucas came even with Slocum. "That doesn't mean we're splitting up. That's not what I was told to do."

"Your pa must want me mighty bad," Slocum said.

When Lucas laughed like a hyena, he almost reached over and caught the man by the throat to choke answers out of him. Deutsch rode just far enough away so that wasn't possible.

"We got a chain of command. Me and Timothy, we do what we're told. It's worked out real good up till now. Never shoulda killed that lawman in Denver. That's what got the Lockes so hot for our hides."

The distant report from rifles grew closer. Slocum heard the shrill whistle of a bullet ripping past. It was way high and no threat, but the rifleman would get in range soon enough.

"How are we going to get across the Rio Grande?" he asked.

"No way we can make the gorge bridge 'fore they catch up with us." Lucas Deutsch pointed toward the southwest. "There's a way down into the gorge I know. We can cross the river there and be on our way."

"They'll shoot us like clay pigeons," Slocum said. All he wanted was the chance to get away from the Deutsch brothers. Clear of them, he could lose the posse, too.

Lucas stuck like glue to him, riding knee to knee. When he changed direction just a mite, Lucas cut him off and herded him back the way he had ordered.

"Ahead, Lucas, there's the notch ahead!" Timothy waved wildly.

Whether the gunshot in the gut betrayed him or he just lost his balance, Timothy Deutsch toppled from horseback and landed in a heap on the ground. Lucas shot Slocum a dirty look, then galloped to help his brother.

Slocum saw the notch in the rocky terrain Timothy had headed for, but he turned his Appaloosa due south so he could ride parallel to the river. The river curled about ten or fifteen miles farther south. Slocum could decide to cross there or keep riding south toward Santa Fe. Whatever he did freed him of the Deutsch brothers and got him away from the posse. They had to split up when Lucas got his brother back on the horse and ran for their way across the river.

The handful of posse remaining wouldn't be hard to lose once he reached the wooded area a couple miles off.

Only the posse didn't split up as he'd expected. If the temporarily deputized lawmen had any sense, two-thirds of them would have gone after the Deutsch brothers and the rest after Slocum. He could lose four men unskilled in tracking.

Only they all kept after him as if he'd had a big red bull's-eye on his back. He would never make the shelter of the woods and the diversion promised there. Cutting back east allowed the posse to cut him off. That left only one direction, and he hated to take it. Slocum rode west again, hunting for the rocky notch that marked the ford where the Deutsches intended to get over the Rio Grande. He couldn't fight off a dozen men. If he led the entire posse back onto the Deutsches' trail, the two outlaws would fight rather than surrender.

Slocum rode hard and felt his Appaloosa begin to falter from exhaustion. He slowed. By now the posse's horses were tuckered out, too. If they had been fresh, he would have been lassoed within a mile.

He saw Lucas and Timothy disappear through the rocky vee in the canyon rim and knew he had spotted the retreat. Slowing a bit more rested his horse but allowed some of the posse to close the gap between them. His hand brushed over the ebony handle of his six-gun. Even if it had been loaded, shooting wildly wouldn't have gained him anything. He was a sharpshooter, but riding a galloping horse, shooting over his shoulder—luck came into play far more than skill.

Right now his luck was wearing a trifle thin.

He chanced a look behind and laughed without humor. The two most aggressive in the posse had run their horses into the ground. The animals stumbled and then pulled up. They might be lame or just pushed past the point where they refused to be ridden one step more. Slocum didn't care. He burst through the rocky doorway and saw the steep path down the side of the gorge.

The Deutsches had already reached the bottom almost a hundred feet down and fought the swift current to reach the far side. The gorge wall there lacked a path, but Slocum guessed the outlaws had only a mile or two ride along the river before the gorge petered out entirely and opened up on level land. They didn't have to risk being shot off the far wall scaling a steep trail.

Slocum intended to overtake them—with a reloaded pistol.

He worked his way down the trail with more switchbacks than he could count. Every time he passed under the notch, he craned his neck up to see if the posse had come through. He gave the Appaloosa its head, letting it pick out the best track and pace so he could fumble in his saddlebags for ammunition.

Trying to reload as the horse swung to and fro on the narrow path proved a chore almost beyond his ability. More than one cartridge slipped from his fingers to tumble onto the rocky trail, but by the time he reached the riverbank, he carried a fully loaded six-shooter.

He started to cross the river when a shot rang out. Then another and another. Close. He looked up and saw three of the posse with rifles aiming downward at him. He pressed close to the gorge wall, cutting off their line of sight.

It was almost twenty yards across the river. With steady hands and sharp eyes, the snipers would cut him down before he got halfway.

He studied the bank going southward. It was rocky and would slow him, even if he got off and walked his horse. Those in the posse not waiting for him to cross would reach the gorge floor eventually and catch him. Any shoot-out put him at a distinct disadvantage. Alone against so many men, he needed a Gatling gun to fend them off.

He had scarcely enough ammo left to reload once the cylinder's six loaded rounds were fired.

The riverbank north looked easier to ride. He knew he couldn't get back up the gorge wall for five miles or better, but maybe the posse might hesitate long enough for him to get across the Rio Grande. As a last-ditch effort, throwing himself into the river and letting it buffet him all the way south offered itself up.

He began riding north, pressed against the rocky wall and listening to at least five in the posse make their way down after him. Slocum doubted he would get out of this alive, but surrendering so Judge Locke could hang him never entered his mind.

17

Slocum rode until he came to a slight bend in the river. The sheer gorge walls prevented anyone seeing him from the rim, and the turn gave a small amount of protection from the posse as they finally reached the bottom. He drew his six-shooter and waited. The rush of the river muffled the sound of his nervous horse pawing at the rocky ground, but it also hid the sound of the posse coming for him.

He forced himself to remain calm as the time stretched from seconds into minutes. When none of the posse came hunting for him, he found himself uncharacteristically anxious. Slocum secured the reins on a rocky outcrop and then edged around the bend to get a look at the base of the trail. What he saw made him jump in surprise.

"There's no need to gun me down. In fact, if you tried, it would draw the entire posse back this way," Marta Deutsch said. She stood with her horse's reins in one hand, her other on a flaring hip. "Sounds carry up and down the river. Trapped by the high walls, you know." She made a sweeping gesture, but Slocum kept his eyes fixed on her.

"Where'd you come from?"

"Why, I was with the posse. After I rode down the trail, I sent them scurrying downstream."

"Why?"

"I happened to be in town when Judge Locke formed the posse and—"

"Why did you decoy them away from me?"

"You are a clever man, John," she said. "You didn't ask how I happened to know you hadn't gone downstream or how I waited for you to come creeping out of hiding."

"I wasn't hiding."

"No," she said, smiling broadly. "You were laying an ambush. Not a good one, though it could have been worse." She looked up at the steep trail. "The men with rifles could never catch you in their sights. Keeping close to the walls took away the advantage of them owning the high ground, but you don't have much ammunition."

He said nothing. Marta smiled even more broadly as she reached into a coat pocket and showed him a couple cartridges in her palm. With an easy smooth move, she tossed them to him. Slocum caught the bullets in his left hand. There was no need to examine them. They were the rounds he had dropped trying to reload on his way down the trail. She had not only found and retrieved them but understood that he ran low on ammo.

"Why did you send them on a wild-goose chase?"

"I don't much like men in a posse," she said. "Their intelligence is lowered to that of the stupidest man in it." Tugging on the reins, she moved her horse around where Slocum got a better look at it.

"That's your pa's horse," he said.

Her eyebrows arched. For the first time she found herself at a loss for words.

"It's a paint, the one he rides," Slocum said to spur her on.

"Why, yes, it is. My horse threw a shoe, and I took the one closest at hand in the barn. So to speak." She mounted and pointed farther north up the Rio Grande. "There's a ford a mile upstream. Once across, a trail winds up to the western rim."

"You know the area pretty well," Slocum said.

"I listen to what my brothers say about exploring the entire length of the gorge. This trail, the one you just came down, is the only way to the floor for miles on the eastern side, but there are any number of others on the west face."

"Why?"

He watched her closely. The smile turned into a leer.

"The moment we had in the barn was good, John. Perhaps I wanted more." She openly leered now. "No, that's not true. There's no 'perhaps' to it."

"You spend all your time saving me."

"From my brothers and the law?" She shrugged. "It looks as if it is my lot in life. I don't mind the chore, if there is something big to reward me." The way she looked at him, eyes meeting his, then dipping lower, just under his gun belt, made her intent clear as if her words hadn't.

"How long will the posse hunt for me?"

"Not too long. There is a stretch that is several hundred yards long and straight as an arrow. Even the dimmest lawman will realize you couldn't have ridden that entire length ahead of them and disappeared around the lower bend, but it will take another fifteen or twenty minutes for them to get there and twice that to return."

She put her heels against the paint's flanks and urged it past Slocum. He slid his six-gun back into its holster, looked at the two cartridges in his left hand, then slipped them into his coat pocket. With a single jump, he mounted and rode after her. Marta took special delight in pressing down hard into the saddle to give him the best view possible. He knew she did this on purpose because of the way she coyly glanced over her shoulder now and again.

As suddenly as she had appeared, she turned and splashed into the river. Slocum hesitated, watching as she and the horse fought against the powerful current. When she was more than halfway across, he saw that submerged rocks in the river broke the power of the water. This stretch wasn't as deep either, providing a safer ford. He wasted no time crossing. By the time he reached the western bank, she had already worked her way higher on a trail made almost invisible by wind erosion.

It took the better part of a half hour to reach the western rim. Once there, Slocum chanced a look back down at the raging river. Only yards from the ford the churning river would have swept any rider foolish enough to try crossing. Of the posse he saw no trace.

"Oh, I am sure they have given up," she said, seeing the direction of his stare. "They might think you were swept to your death. If they care, they might follow the river hunting for your body or your horse's carcass. My guess is that they won't care."

"Judge Locke won't believe I'm dead."

"Not without a body," she said candidly.

Water dripped from Slocum's clothing. He couldn't help noticing that Marta's coat and blouse clung tenaciously to every contour of her body. A slight wind evaporated the dampness and made it feel colder than it was. It didn't take a sharpshooter's eyes to see how her nipples hardened into tiny buttons from the chill. She made certain he saw by stripping off her coat and pulling her shoulders back. The blouse clung even more tightly to her body.

"We really do need to dry our clothes."

"You're wet," Slocum said.

"Your eyesight is far better than I thought," she said, "if you can tell from such a distance." She reached down and pressed her hand to her crotch. "You're right."

She sawed on the reins, turned the paint's face, and galloped away. Slocum wasted no time going after her. She angled away from the gorge, riding in the direction of the X Bar X. When he reached a wooded patch, he slowed, then halted to listen hard. He no longer caught the sound of hoofbeats ahead of him. The sound of wood snapping turned him in a new direction. Riding slowly, he reached a clearing where Marta had already cleared off a section of ground, scooped out a fire pit, and built a small tepee of dried branches.

"We need to get dry or we'll catch our death of cold," she said. Rummaging through her saddlebags, she took out a tin of lucifers, struck one, and ignited the wood.

Slocum dropped to the ground and began gathering larger pieces of kindling to add to the fire. In no time the blaze worked its magic on his coat, drying it. He still removed it and laid it out on the ground as Marta watched with interest. She grinned, dropped her coat next to his, then went on to strip off her wet blouse. A stick poking upright in the ground near the fire provided a way to dry it. Slocum slid off his vest, then his shirt.

By this time Marta had wiggled free of her skirt and stood near the fire, clad only in a flimsy muslin shift. She ran her hands over the thin fabric, pressing it wetly against her body.

"Do you think I should be so bold as to let this dry, too? Or should modesty force me to leave it on?"

She faced Slocum. The material hid nothing. Every curve of her body was revealed; every feature of her breasts and privates was as good as seen without the shift. He stepped closer. He dropped his gun belt. Marta stood motionless, a goddess hewn from delicate marble.

"Our coats are wet. We should do something about squeezing out the moisture," Slocum said.

"Squeezing out the . . . moisture," she said, finally moving to him. Her hand pressed into his crotch. Slocum moaned softly as she began kneading the lump growing there. "I like the idea of squeezing it dry." She popped open the buttons and began flexing her fingers around his rigid length. "I think a better way of getting the moisture out is to . . . suck it out."

She dropped to her knees. Her lips lightly touched the

plum tip of his manhood. Then her head bobbed forward, and she took him full length. Slocum's knees went weak in reaction. She sucked and tongued and kissed. Her eager lips delivered stimulation in ways he had never experienced.

He sank lower, Marta following him until he lay flat on his back on their coats. The dampness in the cloth chilled him, but the feel of her mouth ministering to him sent lightning jabs of heat throughout his body. Her fingers stroked the hairy sac tightening under the shaft, and she somehow rubbed her breasts against his legs as she moved about restlessly.

Slocum reached the point where he couldn't stand it any longer. He reached down, caught the shift on either shoulder, and pulled. The cloth resisted movement since it was still wetly glued to her body. He got his fingers underneath and yanked hard. Cloth tore. Marta groaned and moved up his body. Her legs slid along the outsides of his thighs as she opened herself wantonly to him. Slocum yanked hard and tore the muslin away from her upper body. A second hard tug ripped it the length of her body.

She cast the pieces away and rose naked and gleaming in the sunshine above him. Slocum reached up, cupped her firm breasts, and began tweaking her nipples. She threw her head back, face to the sky, so she could press her body forward into his grasp. Palms flattening her tits, Slocum began arching his back.

They weren't aligned properly at the groin. His hardened length stroked between her nether lips. He felt the heat and damp boiling within her. He wanted more. He had to have it.

Reaching behind her, he caught a double handful of ass flesh and lifted her upward. She pressed one hand onto his chest and used her other to position him properly. When he released the upward pressure on her rump, she sank down— and he sank balls deep into paradise.

They both cried out in pleasure at the sudden intrusion. Marta began swaying back and forth, twisting without lifting. The pressures against his hidden shaft built. The softness, the warmth of her core, the way she squeezed down and then released him with her strong inner muscles all built his desires to the breaking point.

He sat up. Her eyes popped open, and she started to object. He shut off any protest with a kiss. Arms around her waist, he swung about so they reversed position, his manhood never leaving her. Looking down into her face now, Slocum saw a flash of irritation. Marta preferred to be on top rather than pinned beneath a man's weight, her legs spread and vulnerable.

His hips twitched. Moved. Slipped back. Shoved forward. Slowly at first, then with more powerful thrusts. As the friction built, it burned away all of Marta's objections.

Her knees rose on either side of him as he thrust vigorously until he no longer had control. The surging lava-hot tide rose within him, made him even harder, and then erupted from his tip. He continued thrusting until he melted away. Then he held himself above the woman's supine body, his chest pressing into hers.

Even with faces just inches apart, he barely heard her whisper, "I didn't know it could be that good."

"Drying out makes it worth getting dunked in the river."

Marta pushed him up, got her arms between them, and forced him to roll over.

"I agree."

"You glad you rescued me again?"

He watched her expression. Playing poker had given him the ability to read a man's mind. He was at a complete loss to know what went on in her head now.

"I wish it could be different."

"What?" he asked.

She sat up and pushed him down as he tried to sit up also.

"Time to go. The posse."

"They are probably halfway to Santa Fe by now." He wondered at her expression when he said that.

"I'm sure they returned to Taos, boasting of how they got the better of you. Chased you from the territory, maybe killed you. They aren't likely to keep on your trail. Posses lack dedication, determination."

Slocum had seen more than a few in his day that employed expert trackers and would follow their quarry through the gates of hell, but he preferred to watch as Marta dressed. She held up the ripped shift, then wadded it up and tossed it into the fire. She stepped into her skirt, then pulled on the dried blouse and finally pointed to her coat.

Slocum silently rolled off it and handed it to her. It was dirty and still wet. She shook it out, then slung it over her shoulder. Marta studied his naked body and an almost shy smile came to her lips. Or was it one of regret? Again Slocum couldn't tell.

"You'd better ride north as hard and fast as you can. There's nothing for you here. Not anymore."

Marta spun, grabbed her saddlebags, and slung them over the paint. She mounted and rode off without a backward glance, leaving him naked on the ground.

Slocum stretched out and let the sun warm him. He felt sleepy and not a little bit lazy, but he shook it off. With economical movements, he dressed, buried the fire, mounted, and rode after Marta.

He had to see if his suspicions were right.

18

Slocum could have lain in the warm sunlight the rest of the afternoon, but he had to fulfill his duty. Marta took his mind off matters, but only for a short while. When she left, memories of Annabelle flooded back, and Tom Harris and even Marshal Donnelly. Marta's father and brothers had to be brought to justice—and maybe more.

The only way Slocum saw that happening was to wring a confession out of them. Timothy might be dead by now with a bullet lodged in his gut, but the giant of a man looked strong enough back in Taos when he and Lucas broke Slocum out of jail. Slocum didn't lie to himself why they had risked their necks freeing him. Marta had made it sound as if they had done the deed so she could be with him again. He doubted that. More likely they had wanted a cat's-paw to divert attention from themselves after planting the evil seed in Byron Locke's mind that he was one of their gang. The Deutsch gang worked on a scheme requiring the law to look elsewhere.

Slocum didn't appreciate it that "elsewhere" was in his direction.

He rode with the sun in his eyes, forcing him to pull down his hat brim. When the smell of burning wood caught his attention, he veered away and into thick woods to find Rory Deutsch's still. The fire under the pot had died down, but the curls of pine smoke still struggled to get through the canopy of limbs above and reach the sky. A quick survey told him Deutsch had left.

Of course he had. He had seen Deutsch in Taos before his boys broke into the jailhouse.

Slocum frowned when he began piecing together bits and pieces like a shattered mirror. When the reflection came to him, he swore.

"Been looking in the wrong place. Dammit, how could I be so dumb?" He started to leave the still, then lingered long enough to load two Mason jars full of the moonshine into his saddlebags. No sense abandoning such fine Taos Lightning.

He trotted to the X Bar X ranch house and saw a rider disappearing to the south. He eased his six-shooter from its holster, then went directly to the house and went inside without bothering to announce himself. He hurried from room to room. Deserted. Running out, he went to the barn. Both the paint and Marta's horse were gone.

"So her horse threw a shoe?" He went to the side yard where a farrier's forge stood, stone cold. It hadn't been fired up in some time.

There might have been a few spare horseshoes made the last time the forge had been fired up, but Slocum doubted it. Marta's horse hadn't thrown a shoe.

He mounted and turned his Appaloosa southward, intent on finding the rider's trail.

Slocum quit for the day when twilight made tracking difficult and gave up entirely an hour after sunup the next day. The trail had gone too cold for him to find. Reluctantly, he turned eastward and headed back toward Taos. He had a powerful lot of convincing to do, and he wasn't sure how to do it. But he'd think of something.

Judge Locke ranted and raved and finally left the Black Hole Saloon, hands jammed into his pockets and looking fierce. From inside, Pete yelled, "Don't you go accusin' my customers 'less you kin make it stick, you . . ."

Slocum didn't know if Pete finished his threat since he ducked back as Judge Locke stormed past. He started to fall in step behind the man, then hesitated when Byron Locke rode up. The judge went to his son and the two of them argued for some time, drawing attention Slocum couldn't handle. Getting the drop on both men would have gone a ways toward settling his problems, but now it was impossible. He recognized one or two of the men listening as posse members.

When the judge stepped away and the deputy sat straighter in the saddle, the crowd surged forward. From the chatter, Slocum knew the deputy wanted several men to go with him. The details were lost in the hubbub. Taking a chance, he stepped out in the street and walked to the saloon's front door. A quick look behind assured him the Lockes were still arguing and paid no attention to anyone else.

Pete looked up from behind the bar. His eyes went wide, then he smiled.

"You ready to take back yer cantina, Slocum?"

"Business good?"

"Better 'n over at my place. The Black Hole's right on the main street."

"But your gin mill's on the plaza."

"Nobody wants to be seen comin' and goin'. Here, well, there's the folks goin' by and a tad of privacy if they want to sneak in and dip their beak in some beer."

"Deutsch still selling you his Taos Lightning?" Slocum

watched the reaction and knew the answer before Pete spoke.

"Cain't say that's so," the man said slowly. "From all I kin tell, ain't jist me he's cut off. We been talkin' 'bout throwin' in together and gettin' a new source."

"If you all stand together, he can't play off one of you against the others."

Pete scratched himself as he nodded.

"That's the way I see it. Now, you thinkin' on standin' behind this here bar again?"

"Not as long as Judge Locke wants to drop a noose around my neck."

Pete relaxed.

"Glad you know that, Slocum. I didn't want to be the one givin' you that bad news."

"What's he saying about me?"

"Well, sir, it's like this." Pete put his elbows on the bar and leaned forward so he was only a few inches from Slocum. "His boy, that hothead deputy, now he says he overheard two of them what killed Tom dealin' you into a robbery down in Santa Fe. A bank."

"So he still thinks I'm one of the Deutsch gang?"

Pete nodded solemnly.

"Nothing I hadn't figured out on my own."

"He's got this bee in his bonnet that you and them's gonna hit the bank in four days, right after the train delivers a load of gold to the vaults."

"Why does he want a posse to ride with him when he can let the Santa Fe marshal know?"

Pete said, "This is personal to him. And to his pa. Wouldn't do to have another lawman kill you or them, not when he thinks you already kilt his brother."

Slocum hadn't considered this link in the Lockes' thinking. If they believed he rode with the Deutsch gang, why not add him to the bank robbery in Denver where a father lost his son and a brother saw his sibling killed?

"You keep the liquor flowing here, Pete," Slocum said.

"Hard to do with supplies runnin' low."

"Come around back." Slocum went to the back room, then pulled down the locking bars Pete had added to keep the door into the alley secure. It took him a few seconds rummaging about in his saddlebags to get out the two quarts of Taos Lightning.

"Lookee there," Pete said, holding up the glass jars to catch the sun. "This is first-rate hootch. You got more of it?"

"Later," Slocum said. "After I clear my name." Coldness settled in his belly when he knew it went beyond that. He had to bring Annabelle's killer to justice, too.

Pete looked sad when he heard that. Slocum knew the man thought it meant there wouldn't be any more of the potent moonshine for him to sell.

Slocum swung into the saddle and rode around the saloon, watching for any hint of the posse that Byron Locke had been haranguing. Seeing a deserted street, he rode straight for the jailhouse. Only one horse was tethered behind. Slocum caught up the reins and led the horse around to the front. This could go easy or it could turn bloody.

"Judge? Come on out."

"What's wrong?" Judge Locke stepped out, ran into the side of his horse, and bounced back. "Why'd you fetch my horse?"

"Step up. We're taking a ride," Slocum said. He held his six-shooter down at his side, but the judge saw the threat.

"You can't kidnap me. You try and I'll scream for help."

"Then you're dead. Come with me, and I'll show you the real killers who gunned down your other son."

"Byron thinks it was you up in Denver. He heard Lucas and Timothy talking."

"They let him eavesdrop and then released him with an earful of lies. I'd have thought you would have figured that out by now. Reckon I was wrong that you or your boy was smart enough to know a lie when you heard it."

Judge Locke turned slightly, his hand moving to a vest pocket.

"You can keep the derringer, but you try to pull it out and I swear your son'll have a judge killer to chase down."

Judge Locke moved his hand from the hideout gun, swung up into the saddle, and glared at Slocum.

"You're making this worse. Kidnapping a federal judge is a serious crime."

"Add it to the list. You want to find your son's killers or not?"

His silence answered as eloquently as words could. Slocum pointed to the road out of town. Locke snapped the reins and trotted away. Slocum kept close and to the side, where he could see if the judge decided to go for the derringer. They soon left Taos behind and rode straight for the Rio Grande Gorge bridge. It was rickety but better than taking the steep trails down to the river and up the far side.

"Where are we going, Slocum?"

"To the X Bar X. We'll have a talk with Rory Deutsch, and you'll see who's the real outlaw."

"Torturing a confession from him isn't admissible in court. Not in *my* court."

Slocum hoped that proof would be obvious without the rancher needing to testify.

"You said Byron overheard them say they were going to rob the Santa Fe bank?"

"He'll catch them. I'm surprised you're not with them."

Slocum didn't argue the point. It was a long ride to the ranch and trying to change the judge's mind without solid evidence was a fool's errand. He just hoped taking Locke to the ranch didn't also become a wild-goose chase.

"The ropes are cutting into my wrists," Locke protested.

Slocum had tied the judge up the night before when he realized he couldn't stay awake all night to prevent him sneaking away. It had been necessary to keep his wrists bound in front of him when the judge tried to shoot him. Slocum had taken the small pistol he had allowed Locke to keep as a token of his truthfulness and saw that keeping him tied up was the safest course of action when they got to the ranch house.

"We're almost there," Slocum said.

"Looks deserted," Locke said. "Let me go. You can have a couple days' head start before my boy comes after you."

Slocum ignored the offer. It might have been better than he'd gotten from a lawman before, but he had killers to catch—and do so with evidence convincing to the judge. He rode forward to the house, keeping a sharp eye out. He expected to see Marta in the house. As his earlier search ended, so did this one. The X Bar X ranch house had an unused look to it.

The horses were gone from the barn, too. The entire place might be a ghost town.

"They've hightailed it," the judge said. "I want to see the Deutsch boys in my court for what they've done, but I need proof."

"All the proof you have I'm one of their gang is Byron overhearing them."

"He'll catch them when they're robbing the bank."

Slocum started to argue, then realized how everything the deputy overheard had worked together. The Deutsches were laying a false trail so Byron Locke would come after him, but Slocum knew there was something more to what the outlaws said.

"What's in the bank before the gold is delivered?"

"I don't know."

"Get off the horse. We're going to wait a spell to see if they return."

"Byron will stop them."

"If they try to rob the bank."

"I don't understand."

Slocum led the judge into the barn and secured him to a

support post. He curried and fed their horses while the judge kept up a steady barrage of invective against him, detailing how Slocum would swing.

Slocum had finished tending the horses, giving them water from a barrel outside, when he saw riders approaching from the south.

"Keep quiet or I'll gag you," he warned.

When the three riders neared, Slocum cut the ropes holding Locke.

"Keep quiet and listen. This time they won't be lying their asses off."

Locke glared at him, then peered through a knothole in the barn's south wall. Slocum watched the riders through a dirty window. His fingers tightened on the butt of his Colt Navy. Taking them would be hard, one against three. He had to time his attack exactly, after the judge heard damning confessions but before they discovered anyone spied on them.

"Don't let your horse drink too much, Timothy," Lucas said. "It'll bloat."

"We shouldn't have rode so hard. My guts are all hurtin'."

"No reason to kill your horse. With what we stole, we can get out of here and go somewhere fancy."

"I want to go to Frisco," Timothy said.

"We agreed on Saint Louis."

"You and Marta agreed on Saint Louis. I heard o' this saloon in Frisco where they let birds fly all over inside, parrots talkin' and cussin' and—"

Lucas swung around, his six-gun flashing from its holster. Slocum slammed the butt of his Colt against the pane and broke it, firing before the first shards fell away. Then all hell broke loose.

Lucas fired constantly, and Timothy grabbed for a shotgun. Slocum kicked hard at the barn wall and fell backward just as a load of buckshot ripped away where he had stood an instant before. A second blast opened the hole even more, giving him a good view of Timothy Deutsch. Slocum fired once, twice, a third time. Each round found the center of the man's body.

"Slocum, he's getting away!" Judge Locke pressed his eye to the knothole to get a better view.

Slocum rolled and got to his feet, running hard to the barn door. He spun around and fired at Lucas's back until the man disappeared. Refusing to stop, Slocum grabbed the shotgun from Timothy Deutsch's limp hands. To his amazement the man hadn't died, even with three more pieces of lead in him. Finding the box of shells in the outlaw's saddlebags, Slocum took out two, broke open the shotgun, loaded, and fired.

The range between him and Lucas was too great for the shot to have any real chance of stopping him. One or two pellets might have ripped by the fleeing man, but if so, they only urged him to greater speed.

Slocum started reloading, then froze when he heard a rifle round snug into its chamber. Judge Locke had taken a rifle from Timothy's saddle sheath and held it on him.

"He's getting away," Slocum said.

"I've got you. Drop your piece."

Slocum had slipped only one cartridge into a chamber. He had to get the cylinder in place, turn, and fire. With a loaded rifle pointed at his back, he had no chance of winning this fight.

"What's on the pack horse?" he asked.

"Supplies. I don't know."

"Look, Judge. I'm not going anywhere." From the corner of his eye he saw Locke move to the third horse and pull back the canvas protecting the load.

"Son of a bitch. These are gold coins! Bags of them. But Byron said they weren't going to rob the bank for another day."

"The train slows down as it goes through Apache

Canyon. Smart robbers would jump aboard and rob the train there. Why worry about busting into a bank vault?"

"Why not decoy all the law into laying an ambush at the bank and be safe during the robbery?" the judge said in a choked voice.

"Leastways, your son's not going to get into a gunfight. The robbery's already over."

"You could still be one of the gang."

"I'd plug Lucas, too. One of them killed Annabelle."

"Your woman," Judge Locke said, lowering the rifle.

"One of them," Slocum said, "who didn't ride back with these two owlhoots." He looked southward where Lucas Deutsch had ridden.

The third gang member must have been trailing behind while Lucas and Timothy rode back to the ranch.

"Can you catch him? Lucas Deutsch?"

"If you're letting me go," Slocum said.

"I make my share of mistakes. Thinking you were part of the gang is one of them, all because Byron said . . ."

"You stay with him. Don't know there's anything you can do for him unless you want to put him out of his misery." Slocum reloaded as he watched Timothy Deutsch weakly thrashing about in the dirt. He considered putting a bullet in the man's head, then decided he wanted him to die—after a considerable bit of suffering. Timothy Deutsch might not have shot Annabelle Harris in the back, but he sure as hell had a part in killing Tom Harris.

"I ought to get the gold back to Taos, where it can be put in the bank."

"You stay put so I know where to find you. Out on the trail, you're a sitting duck."

"For once, I'll take your advice, Slocum. And, Slocum, watch your back out there."

Slocum laughed ruefully. He had won a small battle convincing Judge Locke of his innocence. Now he had to fight not only Lucas but the real brains of the Deutsch gang.

19

Lucas Deutsch did not try to hide his tracks. He fled from the ranch with one idea only in head: to stay alive. This made Slocum's job easier since the smallest tricks to hiding the trail would have slowed his pursuit. As it was, Slocum overtook Lucas within an hour.

The outlaw rode east through a canyon that opened onto the Rio Grande. The river here split level terrain rather than slashing through a hard-rock mountain and having an 800-foot gorge around it.

Slocum slowed his Appaloosa, put his hands to his mouth, and yelled, "Give up, Deutsch! Your brother's dying. You'll never get away. There's a posse on your heels."

He waited to see how the outlaw reacted. Lucas would never give up from a single shouted threat. He had ridden this way for a reason, and Slocum knew it. Lucas wasn't the brains of the outfit and had to ask what to do next.

The echoes had barely died from Slocum's order to halt when Lucas veered to the left and went directly for the river. He was on level ground now and able to ride faster. Slocum took his time getting through the canyon and to the banks of the fiercely flowing water. Lucas had reached the far side, telling Slocum this was a suitable ford.

He waited until Lucas vanished before crossing. For all his caution, he still almost died. He thought the robber had been spooked enough to ride hard and not do the sensible thing. Slocum was wrong. Halfway across the river Slocum ducked involuntarily as a bullet sang past his ear. His reaction almost unseated him and sent him floundering down the river.

He had entered the swiftest running part of the river. To go back invited a bullet in his back, but he couldn't see where Lucas sniped from. Even if he had, struggling to keep his horse moving in the river took all his skill. He had no way to return fire accurately enough to give himself a few minutes more to reach the eastern riverbank.

Another shot and then another. Slocum winced as the second nicked his arm. Then the river washed away blood and hurt. He angled away from a direct route and let his horse rest a mite as the river helped push them along. He quickly found this was a trap but had no way to avoid it. The bottom fell out of the river here, robbing the horse of footing and forcing it to swim. Slocum kicked free and clung to the saddle horn. Inch by inch he saw the distant shore change as he and the Appaloosa were carried farther downstream, trapped in the current's powerful grip.

The only bright spot came when Lucas no longer wasted ammo trying to kill him. Slocum let himself be battered against the side of his horse until an eddy current pulled them toward shore. Then he pulled himself back into the saddle and got the horse to shallow water along the eastern shoreline.

The horse stumbled as it lost footing in the mud, throwing Slocum. He clung to the reins for dear life. He was about done in, but he knew if he lost his horse, he lost his life. The horse dragged him a few feet before stopping. Slocum caught at the horse's front leg and used this as a crutch to stand. Once he got his feet under him, he grabbed the saddle horn until he regained his strength.

Walking slowly, keeping the horse as protection against new attack, he finally reached a sandy patch and collapsed. If Deutsch had seen how he fought the power of the river and escaped, he would be a goner now. Slocum was too weak even to lift his three-pound six-gun. But Lucas had been too frightened and must have rushed on, thinking his pursuer had died in the river.

Slocum would show him.

He heaved to his feet and walked his horse to a spot where he could study the cottonwoods that Lucas had fired from. To his surprise, Lucas hadn't ridden away when he had the chance. The outlaw sat with his back against a thick tree trunk. His rifle leaned against a dead limb to one side.

Slocum drew his six-gun, wiped off the mechanism the best he could, then knew he had only one chance at capturing Lucas Deutsch alive. Delivering him to Judge Locke wouldn't be as satisfying as shooting him outright, but knowing a rope would be tightened around his neck before the gallows trap opened would do.

He emptied the cylinder, dried each bullet, and examined it, then replaced them. The click as the cylinder fell into place and he cocked the pistol brought Lucas to his feet and grabbing for his rifle.

Slocum fired one round that went wide. Lucas snatched up the rifle and fired wildly. Slocum's second round would have hit right in the bread basket but water had turned the cartridge into a dud. The dull metallic click as it fell emboldened Lucas.

"You were supposed to die in the river, Slocum. What are you? A cat with nine lives?"

"All I need is one to end yours," Slocum said. The third round fired, forcing Lucas to cover. "You can surrender and stand trial. You might beat the charges."

"What happened to Timothy?"

"As hard as I've tried to kill him, the son of a bitch keeps hanging on. He took four of my bullets and he's still alive." Slocum circled to get a better shot at Lucas, but the outlaw had the tree trunks to use as cover. "Might be I just let you go if you tell me who killed Annabelle Harris."

"Wasn't me!"

"Then who?"

Lucas laughed hysterically. "I stopped the deputy and told him you'd shot the bitch. But I didn't do it."

"Your pa? Did he do it?"

Slocum threw himself flat on his belly as Lucas edged around a cottonwood and got off three quick shots.

"Did your pa shoot her in the back?" Slocum shouted to distract Lucas. He rolled and found cover behind a large log. The entire area was a flood plain but the river was lower this year and hadn't overflowed its bank, not for several years, from the look of the persistent vegetation. The tree had been felled long enough ago to be dried out.

The huge chunks of wood that flew away as Lucas methodically fired into it told Slocum the log would be his death unless he found more secure shelter from the hail of bullets.

"I'll shoot your horse, Slocum. Then you'll be on foot and won't ever catch me."

"Kill that horse and I swear I'll walk barefoot through hell to find and torture you to death. The Apaches taught me a whole lot about what makes a man beg for death and how far to go without giving it to him."

"You're lying!"

Lucas stepped from behind the tree and pulled his rifle to his shoulder. He fired at the same instant Slocum did. Both hammers fell on punk rounds. Lucas panicked and tried to lever in a new round instead of ducking for cover.

Slocum's next bullet caught him in the leg and sent the outlaw tumbling to the ground. Lucas grabbed his thigh and screamed in pain.

Slocum closed the distance between them and fired as Lucas reached for his rifle. The slug whanged off the metal receiver and ruined it for anything more than use as a crutch.

He stood over the outlaw, lining up the sights to make a killing shot.

"No, Slocum, don't!"

"He's right, John. You shouldn't. If you kill Lucas, I'll be forced to shoot the deputy."

"It won't be the first time you'll have killed someone, will it, Marta?"

She laughed. The sound was musical, mingling with the flow of the river, the buzz of insects in the still flood plain, and her brother's harsh breathing.

"You are clever, John, but I diverted that cleverness long enough. We made off with a lot of gold from the train robbery. Enough for me to live comfortably for a very long time. The Denver banks and trains simply weren't profitable enough. Another death or two isn't going to stop me from spending it."

"Kill him, sis!"

"Shut up, Lucas. You screwed up everything. Where's Timothy? And your share of the gold?"

"We went back to the ranch to find Pa. He wasn't there, but . . ."

"But Slocum was," she finished for him. "Is Timothy dead?"

"He says not, but he's such a goddamned liar!"

"Your brother's alive, but he's got three more ounces of lead in his gut."

"And you stashed the gold somewhere?"

"Judge Locke's got it," Slocum said. "He's got the gold and Timothy."

"How convenient. I had wondered what I might swap the deputy for. Now I know."

Slocum glanced away from the fallen Lucas Deutsch to where Marta stood a dozen yards away. She had emerged from a thicket, leading a horse with a man draped over the saddle.

"Yes, John, it's Byron Locke. He is such an impetuous man, and so trusting. He thought he was coming to my aid. But then, so did you.

"First of all, send Lucas over to me. Then we can make a deal that returns Timothy and the rest of the gold so we can get out of your hair."

"No."

"Come, come, John. It's not up to you to dicker. Let Judge Locke decide what to do about his son. Otherwise, you'll have a federal deputy marshal's blood on your hands." Her voice turned cold and convinced him she wasn't bluffing.

"If I let him go, what's to keep you from killing me?"

"Now, John, I don't want to do a thing like that. You and I were so good together. I felt it. I am sure you did, too. At least you didn't complain either time."

"Locke won't turn over Timothy. He likely won't give up the gold either, even for his son—the son you haven't killed."

"Yet, John, the one I haven't killed yet. The robbery in Denver would have been bloodless if it hadn't been for that deputy trying to be a hero. I didn't have any choice but to shoot him down. Just as I'll do this one if you don't deal."

"Timothy isn't going to make it. He might be dead by now," Slocum said.

"That's true, sis. I saw Timothy catch at least two slugs in the gut, real near where the first one went in. The way he complained so much, I don't think he's gonna survive the first bullet."

"You're probably right, Lucas. I saw the way he acted when we stopped the train. He wasn't his usual brutish self. Very well, John. I'll swap the deputy for that sad son of a bitch at the business end of your six-shooter."

"What about the gold? You split it three ways? Two-thirds of it is in Judge Locke's care now."

"I am quite good at poker. You can't win every pot. I'll

let the law take this one if I can fold my hand and keep what's left on the table."

Slocum edged around so he could see Marta but keep his six-gun trained on her brother. She held a sawed-off shotgun to Byron Locke's head. The slightest twitch would blow the man's head to bloody mist.

She eyed him with some appreciation.

"It takes quite a man to bring down the Deutsch gang," she said. "If, as you say, Timothy is dead, or at least no good to me anymore, that leaves an opening. Ride with us, John. Join us. Join me!"

"Marta, no, you can't do this," cried Lucas. "He's ruined everything for us. He's—"

"I say who rides with us and who doesn't. It was only chance that you and Timothy were my brothers and were handy. At first. Now I'm not so sure about you."

"Marta, stop saying things like that. Me and Timothy have done everything you asked. It made us rich!"

Marta Deutsch moved around the horse where Byron stirred sluggishly as he lay draped over the saddle. Slocum knew there was only one outcome. He lifted his pistol and fired. The first round went off with a satisfying *pop!* The second was another dud.

The first shot was all that counted. He had caught Locke's horse in mid-chest and brought it to its knees. Even as the horse struggled, thrashing about, Slocum knocked out the spent and dud rounds in his Colt, reached into his pocket, and took out the pair of bullets Marta had retrieved from the trail leading to the floor of the Rio Grande Gorge. He slipped those in.

Lucas Deutsch bowled him over from behind, knocking him flat as Marta cut loose with the shotgun.

"Dammit, Lucas, you got in the way!"

Slocum lifted his pistol. Two shots. That was all he had. The first one caught the fleeing Lucas high in the back just under his shoulder blade. The outlaw stumbled forward to knock his sister to the ground. Slocum came to his knees and aimed as best he could. He fired again. The second round—his last—caught Lucas in the other shoulder. Marta threw her arms around him and the two sat heavily on the ground, her left arm cradling him and her right struggling to lift the shotgun.

"Don't," Slocum said. "I don't want to shoot but I will!" He cocked the six-shooter, knowing the hammer would fall on an empty chamber.

His bluff worked.

"We've got ourselves a Mexican standoff, John," she said. "If I shoot Locke with my second barrel, you can fill me and Lucas full of holes."

"That's right," he lied.

"What say my brother and I leave? I don't kill the deputy and you don't kill us?"

Even as she spoke, she pushed her brother away so she could roll up to her knees and then stand. The shotgun wavered but aimed close enough to Locke to put him in a world of hurt if she fired. She bent, grabbed Lucas by the collar, and pulled him to his feet with surprising strength.

"Good-bye, John. We would have made one hell of a team." Marta backed away with Lucas leading the way.

The outlaw whistled and his horse trotted after him. In a couple heartbeats, the sound of retreating horses echoed through the tiny stand of cottonwoods. Then only silence reigned.

Slocum let out breath he hadn't even known he had kept sucked into his lungs. The six-gun dropped, then he tucked it into the holster as he went to Byron Locke.

The deputy stared up at him.

"You should have shot them. Both of those snakes."

"Sorry about your horse," Slocum said. He had to dig down in the soft earth to free the deputy's leg pinned under the horse's dead weight.

"Why didn't you shoot? I'm nothing to you." The deputy stared hard at him.

"After she took you hostage, what did you hear?"

"You aren't part of the gang."

"That's why I have to get you back to Taos, to tell your pa. He pretty much knows it, but hearing the words from your lips will seal it."

"We're not going after them?"

Slocum lifted his six-shooter and fanned the hammer six times, each time falling on a spent chamber.

"You bluffed her?" Locke's eyes went wide. "I never saw anything like that in all my born days."

"You hurt bad?" Slocum asked. He helped the deputy to his feet. "With a horse as tired as my Appaloosa is right now, it might take a week to get to Taos."

The metal click of a rifle being cocked froze Slocum. He looked up—and down the barrel of a Winchester.

20

"Do we shoot him or hang the varmint?"

"Wait, hold on," Locke said, pushing Slocum to one side and hobbling between him and rifleman. "You know me, don't you?"

"We're rescuin' you from this here murderin' son of a bitch."

Slocum saw others in the posse filtering through the stand of trees, all with rifles pointed in his direction. If one sneezed or mistook any movement he might make for an attack, he would have more holes in him than a pair of woolens left to the moths.

"He's a legal deputy. My pa, Judge Locke, deputized him," Byron Locke said.

Slocum remembered when that had happened, even if it did skirt the truth a mite. Since then the judge had swung back and forth thinking he was a road agent and killer more times than a Regulator clock pendulum.

"He saved me from the real outlaws." Locke pointed in the direction taken by Marta and her brother. "You can overtake them. Lucas Deutsch has a couple bullets in him Slocum put there rescuing me."

The man sighting down the barrel of the rifle blinked. Slocum took that as a good sign. Then he lowered the rifle and waved, "That way, boys. We got crooks to catch and a reward to claim!"

The entire posse galloped off before Slocum could ask for one of their horses—not that he expected any man among them to willingly give up his mount. It still left him and Locke to share one horse.

"Reckon this means we go back to town," Slocum said, "unless you want to walk and let me join them."

"Could be I take your horse and let you walk back to Taos," the deputy said. From the crooked smile, Slocum knew he was joshing. As bunged up as Locke was, he couldn't fight his way out of a wet paper bag, much less shoot it out with Lucas and Marta Deutsch.

"I don't see you have much ammo," Slocum said.

"They took all I had when she caught me. Snared me real slick, too. I was feeling low about guarding a bank that'd never have anything in it to rob. She rode up bold as brass and we got to talking."

"Then you realized she had saddlebags full of gold coins from the train robbery."

"Something like that, Slocum, something like that."

Slocum knew then that the deputy had never suspected Marta until she had the drop on him. He didn't fault the lawman for that. She had pretty much pulled the wool over his eyes, too.

His willing eyes, he amended. Admitting such a lovely filly was evil to the core didn't come easily.

"I have a horse and no ammo. You've got an arm that looks all busted up, not to mention a leg that got twisted when the horse fell on you."

"*My* horse, which you shot. You're going to buy me another one."

"But I've got the only horse around, so we ought to make our peace with one another."

Byron Locke had already thrust out his hand. They shook. Then they got on the trail back to Taos.

"Don't know how I can make it any more legal, Slocum," Judge Locke said. He blotted the ink and handed over the document.

"Never got a piece of paper signed by a judge saying I hadn't committed any crimes," Slocum said. He folded it and tucked it into his coat pocket. "Not sure anybody would believe it."

"I don't think anybody reading that would either, but if you're in Taos, folks will know." Judge Locke looked hard at him. "Don't try to pass that off as a pardon for any crime you might have committed before coming to New Mexico Territory."

"What crime?" Slocum tried to sound innocent and failed. The judge snorted and shook his head.

"My boy's on the mend. Doc Zamora fixed him up real good. Won't even lose use of his gun hand."

"Not sure that's a good thing," Slocum said.

"It is. We still got two of them varmints to catch."

Slocum settled in a chair and tried to figure out what thoughts darted behind the judge's cold eyes.

"What about Rory Deutsch?"

"Him? He's not guilty of anything but extortion, beating on a few saloon keepers, and making the vilest whiskey this side of the Big Muddy. Taos Lightning, indeed."

"You're sure he had nothing to do with the Denver robbery?"

"I asked around. He was in town expanding his moonshine empire. He's not got the spine to actually hold up a bank, not like his young'uns. Extortion and moonshining are his crimes of choice."

"It gnawed at the back of my mind, but I sort of knew that a long time back. He couldn't make a go of the X Bar X so he fired up a still and set out to corner the market in whiskey."

"I asked a couple of his former wranglers. That about sums it up. His wife died a couple years back and all the heart went out of him. About that time, his children took to robbing stagecoaches and then worked their way north into Colorado and banks."

"And trains," Slocum said.

"They were an ambitious bunch."

"Marta Deutsch was," he said. "She was the ringleader. I thought that paint she rode was her pa's because they're both about the same height. Wearing a duster, it's hard to tell more. She made an excuse about her horse pulling up lame."

"Lame excuse," Judge Locke said. "The posse'll fetch her and Lucas back anytime now."

Slocum wasn't so sure. He got to his feet and said, "I'll be at the Black Hole."

"Knock back a beer for me. I'll join you when I finish this report that's going to the district judge."

"Be sure to spell my name right," Slocum said. The judge laughed. Slocum wasn't kidding.

He wandered through the winding Taos streets until he came to the adobe building that was the Black Hole Saloon. His saloon. He went in and saw a good crowd had already entered.

Pete waved to him from behind the bar.

"That 'shine you brung me's about all gone. You git me more?"

"I've been thinking on this," Slocum said. "Why not fire up your own still?"

"Brew my own pizzen?" Pete scratched his chin. "Tried that but the Deutsch boys busted it up and threatened me."

"They won't be back to bedevil you," Slocum said.

"Heard tell Rory Deutsch is out on his ranch but he shut down his still. That cut off our whiskey supply."

"When his boys are brought to justice, there's no reason for Deputy Locke not to go after him for trying to corner the whiskey sales in town." Slocum took the beer Pete slid in front of him. It went down frothy and cool and about the smoothest he had ever tasted. "Where does Doc Zamora get his alcohol?"

"Him? Don't know. Buys it somewhere else since he don't come in here."

"He uses it to clean his instruments. Might be he makes his own. If he does, that means he knows how to run a still, even if he doesn't call it that."

"You're just brimmin' over with ideas, Slocum."

"I've got another one. How much money do you have in the till?"

Pete turned wary.

"I ain't stealin' from you."

"How much?"

Pete pulled out a crate and began pawing through it, counting. Then he looked up.

"Couple days' take here. Almost two hundred dollars."

"The Black Hole is yours in exchange for what's in that box," Slocum said.

"You ain't joshin' me?"

Slocum searched through the clutter behind the bar, found a piece of paper and some ink. He scratched out a bill of sale, signed it, and passed it over.

"The Black Hole Saloon is yours."

"That makes me the owner of *two* gin mills."

"You're going to be the robber baron of Taos. Here and the Santa Fe Drinking Emporium are the foundations of your empire."

"If I kin find me a fellow who kin run a still, I kin take over supply from Deutsch."

Slocum looked to the door when Byron Locke poked his head inside.

"Posse's back. They got 'em, Slocum. They got both of them."

Slocum stuffed the money from the saloon into his pocket, finished his beer, and nodded in Pete's direction. The barkeep stared at the bill of sale, pleased as punch.

"You got them in the hoosegow?" Slocum asked the deputy.

"Undertaker's got Lucas. Looks like your bullets finally killed him. They said he was white as a bleached sheet from lack of blood. That's how they found him. The blood trail."

"Marta Deutsch? She's dead, too?"

"Looks like," the deputy said. "They found her horse near a bluff overlooking the river. She must have tried to escape going down a trail too narrow for the horse, slipped, and fell into the Rio Grande."

"But her body?"

"Swept away. Somebody downstream'll find her in a few days or a week. I'm heading out to the X Bar X to bring in Rory Deutsch for all he's done here in town."

"Good idea," Slocum said. "He used his children to run all the whiskey peddlers away."

"He's responsible for more 'n one killing, less I miss my guess. I'll find out."

Slocum's mind wandered as the deputy rambled on about how he and his pa would clean things up, then install a new town marshal.

"I'm riding on," Slocum said. "Can you tell me where Marta Deutsch went over the cliff?"

Byron Locke blinked at this, then scratched out a map in the dusty street.

"Obliged, Deputy."

Slocum walked away, not wanting to get into a long discussion with the lawman. He had run his race in Taos. It was time to move on.

Slocum mounted his Appaloosa and put ten miles behind him before the sun sank behind the Sangre de Cristo Mountains. Before noon the next day he found the spot where the posse claimed Marta had fallen to her death. Slocum studied the evidence and agreed. Rocks dislodged, earth cut up by horses' hooves, even a bit of fabric from her coat left on a fishhook cactus clinging to the cliff face a foot or so down from the rim.

He swept in a circle, found brush marks in the dirt, and set out due east away from the river.

Slocum found her camp a little after sundown.

He rode up. Marta Deutsch was slow to respond, but when she did, she turned a beautiful, smiling face to him.

"I wondered if you would believe the posse. I overheard them saying they thought I'd plunged to my death into the river." She poked at the cooking fire, then tapped the coffeepot. "You want some coffee, John?"

"Why did you shoot Annabelle in the back?" He dismounted and went to a stump across from the woman.

"So, you don't want coffee. I hope you don't mind if I have some." She poured some into a tin cup and sipped. "Very good."

"Why?"

"I didn't know you then. It was all intended to divert Judge Locke. That man is so single-minded."

"You killed his son. And you shot Annabelle with my gun."

"Both are true, but I didn't mean to cause you any distress, John. I came to know you afterward. It was necessary to send Locke and his son sniffing away in a direction other than . . . mine."

"Your pa never took part in any of the robberies, did he?"

"Oh, I made sure he thought of himself as patriarch, but he's not a bright man. He couldn't even make a success of the X Bar X. The ranch is—or could have been—one of the finest in the Taos Valley. All he wants to do is distill his moonshine." She shrugged. "It isn't a bad racket, but it's so limited."

"But killing folks like Tom and Annabelle Harris and robbing banks and trains—that's not limiting?"

"Oh, no, not if you're smart. I am, John. So are you. Is Timothy dead?"

"Nope. But he'll stand trial and hang."

"That will satisfy Judge Locke's bloodthirstiness," she said, putting the cup down beside her. "I made the offer before. You and me. We can get rich by pulling only the best robberies. No penny-ante banks or trains. Only those with the most gold."

"The way you sent Byron Locke on a wild-goose chase before robbing the AT&SF train was smart."

"You weren't fooled. You wouldn't wait for the gold to be put in a bank vault before stealing it."

"You murdered Annabelle and framed me for her killing."

"I told you, John, that was before I knew you. Let's let bygones be bygones. I won't hold shooting Timothy and killing Lucas against you. So don't hold that woman's death against me."

She went to pick up her cup again. Slocum moved as fast as he ever had, his aim as accurate as he had ever fired. His slug caught her in the middle of the forehead. She died with a smile on her face—and a derringer in her hand. Marta toppled to the side and lay still.

Slocum edged around the fire, keeping a close watch on her. Any ordinary woman would be dead from such a shot to the head. Slocum knew snakes never died until the sun went down. Marta might have some life left in her.

He knelt and opened her saddlebags. They were filled with gold coins from the train robbery. Her share. Timothy and Lucas's share had been turned over to Judge Locke back at the X Bar X. As far as the law knew, all three fugitives from the Denver bank robbery and killing of Locke's son were dead or in custody awaiting trial before being hanged.

Slocum saw no reason to return Marta's share of the train robbery. He had a couple hundred dollars from selling the Black Hole Saloon, but this amounted to a couple thousand.

It didn't come close to making up for Annabelle's death. Nothing ever could.

He slung the heavy saddlebags over his shoulder, stepped back from the corpse, and returned to his Appaloosa. In an hour he was two miles away. By sunrise he had put ten miles behind him. A week later New Mexico Territory was far behind, even as the memories lingered.

Watch for

**SLOCUM AND THE DARLING
DAMSELS OF DURANGO**

419th novel in the exciting SLOCUM series
from Jove

Coming in January!